The
thimble
shoppe

a prairie creek romance

D1523184

ELIZABETH
BROMKE

About this Book

A small-town girl, her wounded lumberjack, and an inbox full of warm memories make for this charming sweet romance from *USA Today* bestseller, Elizabeth Bromke.

When **Mabel Ryerson** opens her social media to find a friend request from her grandmother, the seamstress's simple life screeches to a halt.

Grandma Betty died two years ago.

Mabel suspects the old account must have been hacked. Still, curious to a fault, the thirty-something wants to go home to investigate. But her fiancé forbids it. Relations are strained among Mabel's family, and her groom-to-be thinks it's better that she focus on her new life, away from Prairie Creek and its memories and secrets.

Griffin Dempsey is poised to join his dad at the helm of his family's logging company. Until the senior Dempsey decides to retire in the tropics. But when Griffin's father offers the whole shebang to his son, Griffin hesitates. After all, what is the company without its lovable father-son duo working together? Griffin starts the process of closing up shop, but he's stuck. There's a reclusive investor who still sits on the company's board, and he isn't budging. Griffin would confront the guy, if

Old Man Kimble weren't related to the one who got away.

Can old wounds turn into second chances? Or will Mabel walk down the aisle with someone who isn't part of her painful past? *The Thimble Shoppe* is a sweet, small-town, second-chance romance set in the simple world of Prairie Creek.

Take a trip to the heartlands and fall in love with the townspeople of Prairie Creek in this romantic, Americana-inspired series, where nostalgia for yesteryear meets the modern wonders of today.

Be sure to begin with book 1: The Country Cottage.

For Grandma Engelhard, a prairie girl

June 8, 1960

I think, once you get married, you become someone new. Even now, just hours into my marriage, I can't stop thinking about my name. It's changing, you know.

Yesterday, I was Betty Merkle. Today, I'm...

Elizabeth Marie Kimble

Elizabeth Marie Merkle-Kimble

Mrs. Elizabeth Kimble

Mrs. James Kimble

Mrs. James L. Kimble

Now that I'm married, I wonder if folks will still call me Betty?

Mrs. Betty Kimble.

1

Hard to say, since my mother went by Annie even though her given name was Anne. Then again there was my Aunt Edna who only ever went by Edna. Although, she never married.

If the occasion arises where I'm supposed to introduce myself, I'll just say Betty since everyone, even Jim, still calls me that.

Diary, that's what I'll call you, I am vacillating between thinking about my new name and admiring my new wedding ring. It belonged to my grandmother on my mother's side. It's a beautiful silver ring, a very comfortable fit. On top of it are just about a million diamonds. Well, I counted. There are eleven. Ten small ones and one bigger one in the middle. The little ones twist around the big one, and it's the most fashionable and expensive piece of jewelry I will ever own. I'm sure of it.

Back to names.

My new initials are EMK. Jim's are JLK. It feels regal, the letter K. Or presidential.

Next week, I plan to monogram our bath towels with our initials. I'll do it by hand with the sewing kit my mother gave me for my bridal shower. I'd always just used my mother's olive green kit. It has a little clasp that hardly ever works on account of its age, but I already miss things like that, like my mother's sewing kit. It's nice to have my own, but still. Mine feels empty by comparison!

Inside of Mother's, she keeps her stash as orderly as a seamstress possibly can. There's a compartment for new needles and one for old—when they get to be a certain age they break so fast, she likes to keep them separate. In the bottom goes her seam ripper and fabric scissors, measuring tape, chalk. She used to have patterns and thread in there, but her collection got to be a lot, so now her thread all goes into an aluminum tin. Patterns are kept in the left drawer of the buffet. The fabric hangs like wet leaves over drying racks in her spare bedroom. One day, I'll have a room just for all of my sewing supplies. A girl can dream!

Anyway, I didn't sleep a wink last night, sharing a room with Jim. In my mind beneath the cover of darkness, I went through what I have and what I'll need if I'm to take on all the sewing needs of our new family. It helped keep me from squirming around too much. I'd hate to have woken Jim. I guess there's a lot that changes when you get married, like being extra quiet at night.

So, here I am. Just married! A newlywed, they call me. I rather like that, because it makes everything feel fresh, and well, that's just what my life is now. I moved from Mother and Father's house into the apartment above Jim's daddy's shop just last night, after the reception. Well, gee— there I go with the "I" this and "Me" that. I meant to write "We" moved into the apartment, Jim and I. We're a "We" now, you see. Gee!

It's a little strange waking up in the same room as a man, even if he's my husband. Jim was bashful about the whole thing, too. We sort of woke up at the same time, I think, because when I opened my eyes, I was looking straight at Jim, who looked as though he'd just opened his eyes. We sort of smiled at each other. I wanted to say,

"What now?" I wanted to giggle. But Jim seemed to know what to do. He cleared his throat and got out of his bed then made it up quickly—Army corners and all. Then he sort of adjusted his Long Johns and looked all shy and said, "Won't you excuse me?"

I just pulled the covers tighter under my chin and nodded, giddy as a schoolgirl.

Once Jim was safely in the bathroom, I unbraided my hair and felt foolish for having braided it last night. Maybe married women don't "do braids" anymore. It's as though I've lost all memory of what my own mother does. Oh, yes. Curlers. I'll have to see about those now that I'm a Married Woman.

Gee!

Anyway, Jim has gone downstairs to open the shop. Did you know he's taking over his daddy's shop? Of course you don't. You're a brand-new diary. Anyway, the shop is called Kimble's Shoppe. Jim's daddy and mother have run it since they married. Mr. Kimble has always done the vacuum servicing, and Mrs. Kimble offers simple mending, hemming, tailoring, and even laundry, wash-and-fold. It's a big job!

Mrs. Kimble is how Jim and I met, as you might recall from my previous diary. Or maybe you don't. Anyway, Mrs. Kimble and my mother sew together on Sundays with the First Faith Presbyterian Ladies Circle. When we moved to Prairie Creek this past winter, the two mothers set about matchmaking. They were right! Jim and I make quite a match.

Now that Jim is wed (to me!), he takes over for his daddy down below. He plans to change the name to something clearer, like Kimble's Laundry 'n' Sew. Something like that. Anyway, I think I'll also start working in the shop, but all of that will come in time. For today, I'm to settle us into our new home. Mother and Mrs. Kimble are coming over for lunch, and they'll help me make decisions on just about everything from curtains to placemats. After that, we'll go together into Aberdeen to the Fabric Barn to make our purchases. Jim has given me a small budget, and this shopping trip will really test it!

Well, I suppose that's all for now. Time to get ready for my first real day as a Wife!

Good-bye!

Sincerely,

Mrs. Betty Kimble

Chapter 1 — Griffin

Griffin Dempsey emerged from his work shed out back, his hands raw from changing out the disc on the stump grinder he'd brought home from work. He didn't mind bringing work home, especially when it came down to machinery. He'd even driven home an excavator before and changed the oil filter right there, just outside of his two-car garage. It was the computerized machines at work that he'd shied away from. All Griffin needed to be happy was a workshop, a box of tools, and some grease.

He stopped first in the mudroom at the back of his house, where he washed his hands with Fast Orange and dried them with shop towels.

Sam snored on the wood floor, where he liked to nap near the cool breeze that wafted in through the screen door.

"Hey, Sammie Boy," Griffin half-whispered at the old hound. "Wake up. It's time for breakfast."

Sam might be on in his years, but his hearing and smarts were sharp as ever. His sagging eyes perked up and his tongue slipped out the side of his mouth and he hefted his squatty body up and waddled after Griffin in through to the kitchen, where Griffin set about putting on eggs and bacon, and digging into the dog food bag for a bowl full of kibble for his best pal.

Coffee percolated near the stove, and Griffin glanced at the calendar he had pinned to the front of the pantry. It wasn't fancy, but he liked things that way: simple. Easy. Keeping track of appointments in his phone felt like more work than it was worth, anyway.

Today's date was clear of any and all obligations, save for one big one. His dad's retirement party that evening. The whole company had the day off for the occasion. Fletcher Dempsey's retirement was a milestone for Fletcher and Son Logging Co. The start of a new era, where the loggers and support staff would see Griff rise to the challenge of taking over all operations. Of course, Griff wouldn't be the sole boss. His dad had promised he'd stick around to help. After all, what would the father-son company be without, well, the father? Anyway, Fletcher was young as far as retirees went and full of the vim and vigor still required to run an old-timey operation such as theirs.

Griffin poked the date on his calendar with the pad of his index finger. "Today is the day," he mumbled to himself. On the floor nearby, Sam stopped chowing and looked up. Griffin spoke now to the dog, instead of just himself. "Time to put on our big-boy britches, Sammie Boy. Tonight, everything changes for us. Heck, maybe I'll make you the vice president of operations." Griffin dropped to a knee and gave Sam a good neck scrub, his voice twisting gutturally. "What'd'ya say to that, boy? Huh? Fletcher and *Sam* Logging Company. Has a nice ring, doesn't it? Maybe now I can buy that new mulcher. Nobody loves learning his way around new machines more than you and me, boy."

The big party took place at The Gulch, a watering hole down south of town. It was the only sort of locale to have a party for loggers. Griffin's buddies, Miles and Logan, helped set it up as a retirement gift. Griffin's dad would arrive just after the party had begun as a sort of special appearance. For a set of roughnecks, the guys had done a decent job of getting everything together.

Once most of the company had settled in with a beer and a burger, Griffin returned to his pals at their high top where he could keep an eye out for his dad.

Miles grabbed Griffin's shoulder and gave it a hard squeeze and a shake. "Big night for you, too, eh, Griff?"

Griffin took a pull from his own long neck, the distinct warmth of smugness moving up his neck. Probably making him flush at the cheeks. He tried to distract his friends from seeing him turn red by giving his head of dark waves a shake, forcing them to fall over his face just enough. He wore his hair longer than he ought to, but the wild waves were a nuisance to get right even in the most capable barber's chair. His dad always told Griffin he looked like a hippie punk. His friends said he was clinging to his youth. But Griff didn't much care. He preferred the comfort of longish hair. He could pull it back with a headband on a hot afternoon or wear it down for extra warmth on those frigid winter mornings out in the forest or on the wind-beat prairie. Anyway, he'd only tried a shorter haircut once in the past twenty years. He'd cut it down low for his tenth high school reunion. It didn't do the thing Griffin hoped it would. Instead, he'd just gotten flippant comments that he was barely recognizable. Baby faced. Old looking. All the wrong sorts of comments.

So, Griffin figured that as long as he still had the same hairstyle as he'd had in high school, then, well, he was the same guy he always had been. That's what Griff liked, too. No change. Things just the same. That was Griff.

"There he is!" Logan pointed with his beer bottle wedged between his thumb and forefinger. "The man of the hour!"

In through the door strolled a very different looking man from the father Griffin had expected. Instead of a trucker's hat and Wranglers, cowboy boots and a dusty ol' flannel with a puffy vest over top, Fletcher Dempsey looked like a complete stranger. And on his arm? None other than Griffin's stepmom, a real number of a woman who'd never once made it a point to show up at the office or at the logging base. A woman who was so far removed from the Dempsey men's lives that Griffin sometimes forgot his dad had ever remarried at all.

Fletcher and his newish wife, Tammy, were a sight for sore eyes. She wore a floral dress, skintight and loud, to put it plainly. Her white-blonde hair was feathered into oblivion and her nails glowed pink from the tips of her fingers, pink to match her lips which looked like they could pop at the slightest twitch. Griffin's mother sometimes suggested that Tammy had had work done, whatever that meant. Around Tammy's delicate neck hung a heavy bouquet of flowers—a Hawaiian lei.

Fletcher wore khaki shorts, his pasty white legs sliding down into flipflops—*flipflops!* On top, he boasted a floral button-down to match the decibel level of Tammy's dress. A lei hung around his neck, too.

Miles threw a look at Griffin. "Was this supposed to be a themed party?"

Logan laughed. "I forgot my suntan lotion."

Griffin brushed off their comments and strode to his dad, slipping through a pack of congratulating loggers who'd already started in on teasing the old guy. "Dad, you look *relaxed*," he joked.

Fletcher smiled easily and gave his bride a squeeze and kiss before she slid away to get their drinks. "Son, I have some big news tonight," Fletcher boomed.

"Let me guess," Griffin replied wryly. "You're retiring?"

Fletcher smirked. "I'm retiring, *and* I'm hitting the road, Griff, my boy."

"Oh yeah? Getting out of Dodge for a while to celebrate? Does Tammy think you need a vacation? She's not wrong, I guess." It was all banter and fun, but Fletcher's cheery, ruddy face fell more serious.

"Can I have a word, son?"

"A word?" Griffin turned edgy on the spot. "Dad, come on. It's your party. Let's have a good time. We can talk business later."

"Tammy, um, sprung something on me, Griff. I'll need you at the office first thing tomorrow to handle it." His dad slipped him a piece of paper that seemed to materialize from nowhere.

"What's this?" Griffin studied the words through a frown.

"I'm sorry, son. It's...it wasn't my idea." He laughed nervously and held up both hands and a different crowd emerged, more employees, coming in to shake the big guy's hand and give him a pat on the back.

Griffin found himself alone, reading what could only be a notice of sale.

Fletcher Dempsey didn't want Griffin to take over. He wanted to sell the family business.

Chapter 2 — Mabel

Mabel Ryerson dropped her toothbrush into the glass on the sink. It clinked into place. Mabel winced at the noise. She really needed to get a new toothbrush holder. The sound of glass clinking and tinkling was a source of agitation for her. Some may even call it a trigger, but Mabel wasn't moved to use such new-age terms. Even if she was born a millennial, the thirty-eight-year-old didn't quite relate to her peers and their jargon.

Blowing air up her forehead and spraying out her dark bangs, Mabel left the bathroom and veered directly right into her bedroom to continue her nighttime routine.

First, she turned her bed down, squaring her current cross stitch project on her pillow as she clicked on the bedside lamp. Mabel always had a project going. Now, it was a set of dishtowels for her friend, Lucy. Next, it'd be an afghan for a woman at work. She'd be undergoing chemo, and Mabel figured she'd enjoy something warm. After the afghan, Mabel had grand plans to work on a new dress for herself. She wasn't often a garment maker, but every three or four projects, she tried to fit something in to keep from getting too rusty. Sundresses were simple, and summer was upon her, so—a pretty cotton dress, yellow, would fit the bill wonderfully.

After adjusting the needle that poked out from the project, Mabel left the room for the kitchen to fetch a short glass of just-in-case water, for those rare occasions she woke up in the middle of the night, mouth dry and throat screaming for something to wet it down and cool it. The glass of water wedged between her arm and chest, she grabbed her orange pill bottle and gave it a little shake. One white capsule rolled perfectly into her palm, and she carried that and the water back to her bedroom, where she then turned off the overhead light and downed the pill with one quick swig of water—not enough to make her need to go the bathroom. Just enough to wash down the doctor-ordered dose of snoozing supplements.

Before crawling beneath her freshly washed sheets and weighted duvet, Mabel tapped her phone awake where it lay on her tall dresser. She opened her text messages to find an unread one from Lucas, her fiancé. It was identical to every other goodnight text he sent her every single night. Not even a period was out of place. Not a comma. Not a capital letter. Orderly and predictable, just the way Mabel liked him. Just the way Mabel needed him in fact.

She typed out her equally predictable and orderly reply. *Good night, and sweet dreams. I love you too.* Then Mabel hit send.

That was it. Now it was time for her to slip into bed and read until her medicine stole her off into a land of bad dreams and good.

But a pesky notification persisted on her phone screen. A little red number *One* hovering above her social media messaging app. One she hardly used and therefore had no cause to court messages from.

Mabel tapped the icon, and her inbox appeared. At the top, an unread message, as indicated. Naturally, that wasn't the surprise. The surprise was the sender.

Blinking and squinting at the name, Mabel was afraid to open the thing. It couldn't be.

But there it was, clear as day. A message.

From Mabel's dead Grandma Betty.

Chapter 3 — Betty

October 12, 1960

Well, the cat is out of the bag, as they say. Jim and I are more than husband and wife, we're future parents, too. You read that right. I've just learned I'm pregnant. The doctor even confirmed it this morning. I can't even imagine how my life will change next.

You may recall that my best friend in the world, Bertha, just had her first baby in August. It was quite the excitement in town. There was a beautiful baby shower with soft blues and pinks and yellows. I crocheted Bertha a blanket—cream colored with gray in it. The baby came out a little boy. They call him Fletcher. Fletcher Dempsey. He's the cutest thing in the world, but Bertha has confided to me that it's tiresome work, having a baby. She doesn't sleep much, and Joe isn't so good about helping with the night feedings. Little Fletcher takes a bottle, which Mother had something to say about. Anyway, I suppose Bertha had hoped that since she isn't nursing, Joe might take a feeding, but he has to go to work in the morning of course. Joe is a lumberjack out of town, and his drive alone has him up early.

I tried to remind Bertha that Joe's probably just as tired as she is, but I never should have said a word, because that just made her cry for a long spell.

Well, now that I'm pregnant, I figure I'll come to have my own fits, too. It's only natural, Mother says, for a new baby to bring about a lot of trouble. It will be my job to see to it that such trouble doesn't impose upon my marriage or our home life.

The only problem is that we're already having a bit of trouble. Now that Jim's been overseeing the shop, it seems like we've lost some regular customers. I guess they don't trust the younger generation, because quite a many of the laundry customers moved their business up to Aberdeen or even just took back over on the work themselves.

However, I have an idea that might help. I figure there are certain local businesses that could use a laundry service and maybe also a sewing service. Just think, if I can bring in new customers, then we'll make more money. Once the baby comes, Jim and I will be all set. There won't be much trouble because of all the money we could be making downstairs!

That's my plan, anyway.

Besides the business, life is busy as a wife! I'll tell you

what, cooking and cleaning never tired me out so much before. Maybe it's the baby. He or she sure does wiggle around a lot for being so tiny. Another thing, I've heard a rumor that a pregnant woman's fingers can swell. I'm worried about my wedding ring. Should I have it resized? Or should I store it somewhere for safekeeping? One of many questions I'll have, I'm sure!

My due date, the doctors think, is Valentine's Day. That's right. February 14. Can you believe it? If this baby is a boy, and he comes when he's due, well, we have to name him Cupid!

Jim didn't think that was funny, but I do. I wouldn't really name a baby Cupid. I'll name all of my babies— and I hope I have a lot!—after great people. I like the idea of naming a child for another person. If we have a boy, I think James Junior would be nice. We could call him Jimmy. Or just Junior, even.

For a girl, maybe I'll pick the name of a smart book character. You'll think me silly for this, but I just love those mystery novels, like Agatha Christie ones. Maybe I'll name my baby Agatha, but isn't that old fashioned?

I'll keep thinking...
Until then, Diary.
Sincerely,
Betty (The Mother-to-Be!)

P.S. Did I tell you what Jim got me for my birthday? A Singer sewing machine. It belonged to his mother, and Jim and his father repaired and oiled it just for me. It was quite a generous gift, which is why I had the idea to open a business of my own! I'm a little scared to use it. What if I break it? Well, I guess I'm married to a capable man who can fix it for me! What a luxury!

Chapter 4—Griffin

Let down and irritated, Griffin had left the retirement party as soon as it was respectable. He read and re-read the notice his father had given him. It was an official listing document, stating that a business and its liquid properties were for sale to the highest bidder. Devery Barnaby was the listing agent, someone Griffin had otherwise admired. But small towns were rampant with traitors, even unsuspecting ones.

Why Fletcher hadn't offered to just hand the whole shebang off to Griffin was no mystery. Logan and Miles, who'd left the party with their buddy, agreed:

Tammy was to blame.

She had to be. She'd never been interested in the family and even less so in the logging industry. It made sense she'd want to cash in and move on.

That's exactly what they were doing, and the worst part? Griffin realized just how much he meant to his father. And it was exactly *less* than his new wife meant to him.

"I don't know why anyone gets married anyway," Griffin mused back in his living room, where his buddies were cracking into fresh brews and channel surfing for the best sports option on his limited cable plan. Griffin lifted his own beer at Logan. "Speaking of which. How's Kelly?"

Logan hadn't much talked about the new lady in his life. The whole thing, in fact, was a bit of a secret in town. Sure, Logan had started to introduce her around the town, but not as a girlfriend. Logan was telling everyone that Kelly Watts had retired early and now filled her days helping him overhaul the cottage. They were going to turn it into a real inn. Something more than his ol' Aunt Melba had ever dreamed of.

Miles and Griffin knew the truth, though. Logan was as interested in Kelly as he'd ever been in Delilah.

Maybe more so.

That's where the controversy came in. Reason said that two years was enough time to grieve the loss of a loved one. But reason didn't know Prairie Creek and how much it loved Delilah.

Predictably, Logan brushed off the comment. "She's great. Really helpful. I've never met anyone with an eye for home design like Kelly has." His admiration was palpable and vivid, like he was picturing a starry night and not the woman who was apparently nothing more than a business partner.

"When will you two come out with your relationship?" Miles didn't have much of a filter. Not when it came to romance. A self-proclaimed lifetime bachelor, he enjoyed making the other two bristle about all things coupledom.

Logan moved the conversation seamlessly. "Did you hear Mabel's engaged?"

Tires screeched. Albums scratched. The world stopped. Griffin had enough surprises for one night. He set his beer down on the coffee table and pinned his friend with a look. "No," he replied simply.

Griffin licked his lips and ran a hand over his mouth as Logan and Miles exchanged a look.

"No?" Griffin repeated, this time as a question. "When? Why? To that guy?" The questions could keep tumbling, but he forced himself to shut up. Griffin didn't care about Mabel Ryerson. Not one iota. And he hadn't since they were just kids, either.

"It happened after the funeral, I guess." Logan downed the last of his drink. "Lucas, yeah. The one who came to Melba's funeral." The reason Griffin wasn't invited to the funeral. But the guy was just a boyfriend then. And he used a funeral as a jumping-off place for a *proposal*? Griffin had some choice thoughts about that.

Miles took the opportunity to change course. "Isn't Kelly Watts engaged, too?"

Logan answered easily as he kept his gaze on Griffin. "Not anymore."

"Why did Mabel get engaged?" Griffin had a need to

know this. It made no sense. From everything Logan had said, the Lucas guy was a stand-in. A non-starter. "Mabel's too good for that guy."

"Why do you even care?" Logan gave Griffin a hard look.

Griffin met it. "You know why I care."

Miles joked, "I think you had a chance to care when you were eighteen." They all knew that Griffin had lost his only shot at being Mabel's man. Back then, when she was just sixteen and he was graduating from high school, the world was their oyster. But they were young, even though Mabel thought they were old enough to do something drastic, like elope.

Griffin had disagreed. Not only did he know her parents would never go for signing off on a teen wedding, he also knew what marriage *could* be. And the picture wasn't pretty. Griffin had seen enough failure in marriages around him. His parents. Then his dad with Tammy—*shudder*. Then Logan and Delilah. Although, you couldn't count death as a marital failure.

Could you?

Well, you could if the death was the fault of one of the spouses. But Delilah's death was hardly Logan's fault.

It was hardly even Mabel's fault. But still she acted like it was. And that's exactly why she would never come back to Prairie Creek. Not for anything other than a funeral, at least.

Chapter 5 — Mabel

Mabel ignored Lucas's opinion on the matter of what she ought to do about the strange correspondences. She ignored everything, in fact. Even reasonableness. Instead of sleeping, she finished her cross stitch. She could take it with her. Lucy would be around, no doubt. Might as well get the towels done and handed off so she could get started on the afghan.

Then, instead of getting dressed for work that morning, she pushed her hair into a ponytail, pulled on a pretty floral print dress, and left Lucas's frantic phone calls unanswered. She pulled out an overnight bag and added to it her medications, exactly one outfit—a romper she'd made herself the summer before—and her yarn and crochet hooks. She got in her car.

And Mabel drove home.

It was unprecedented, this return. Well, she had been

back to Melba's funeral just weeks earlier, yes. But as far as casual visits back—or even formal ones—Mabel had personally sworn them off. It was too hard to face people. Logan, most of all. Her parents, too. Though, they were no longer living in Prairie Creek, their presence lingered there. It reeked of memories of her family, that little town.

Melba's funeral was bad enough. That's why Lucas had joined her, to provide a human crutch to her emotional damage. He held her up through the service at First Faith. He drove her to the reception. He stood stolidly by her side throughout the reception, thwarting advancing relatives who wanted to *just talk to Mabel for a moment*. Mabel didn't know what anyone had to say to her. Maybe they wanted to tell her that she was a murderer. That she'd killed two people. Or maybe they wanted to forgive her. But even if aunts, uncles, cousins, and friends had forgiveness to offer Mabel, she didn't want it. Because forgiveness meant that it was real. That what she'd done that day on the icy roads of South Dakota, wasn't a nightmare.

It was reality.

She made a pitstop at the halfway point between Fargo and Prairie Creek. It was a truck stop, which was fine. All Mabel needed was gas, coffee, and internet.

After filling her tank, she ducked into the 24-hour

diner attached to the fill station. A tired waitress guided Mabel to a vinyl booth and when asked for the wi-fi password, pointed to a handwritten note taped on the bottom of a tube TV that hung precariously above the counter.

Mabel found the network on her phone. *Lumberjacks Stop-n-Fill.* The password scrawled on the paper on the TV was the same as the network, except spelled wrong. She tapped it in. *lumberjaxstopnfil.*

It connected immediately, and Mabel was back online. Not that she wanted to be, necessarily. But because she had to.

Before returning to her scarcely monitored inbox, the diner door jangled open and in walked a troop of men in flannel shirts and jeans, full beards and thick arms. Loggers, Mabel knew. The area wasn't necessarily known for forestry operations, but Mabel was all-too familiar with the type. Without a moment's pause, she immediately thought of Griffin. Her first love. Deep down inside, Mabel probably considered him her only love. But one's only love didn't matter in the face of flagrant rejection.

In fact, if there was one thing she dreaded more about Prairie Creek than the brutal memory of the car crash, it was the threat of bumping into Griffin Dempsey. In fact, that fear of seeing him was as emotionally grave a risk as was the fear of facing the demons of Delilah's death. Or Grandma Betty's.

The problem of Griffin had been elevated when he'd

arrived at Grandma Betty's funeral, two years earlier. His very presence was so traumatic that it drowned the effects of the Xanax that had kept Mabel's heart bobbing at just the surface. She'd fled from the funeral and from his sympathetic eyes and told herself that if she'd ever come back to Prairie Creek, she'd make sure she wouldn't have to face him.

Mabel tried to ignore the loggers' presence even as they passed her to sit in a booth at the rear of the diner. Instead, she focused on opening her inbox and combing back through the pages and pages of words that Grandma Betty's account had sent her.

All of them were written as if journal entries. Each with a date, beginning in 1960 and going clear through to 2000, although many years were missing. All told, the entries totaled 7 and each reflected a significant moment in the woman's life.

The implications were either that Grandma Betty had stopped journaling by 2000, she'd stopped having important life moments by 2000, or whoever had sent the messages had stopped at that year. Of course, it could have been that whoever had sent the messages selected certain entries or had access to only the ones he or she had sent.

Regardless, Mabel hadn't realized her grandmother was a writer to this degree. And if these really were Grandma Betty's, then Mabel believed that there was more to their online existence than mistake.

This was no hacking situation. A hacker, having

copied a deceased person's profile, would send a friend request. Or a vague message that didn't ring quite true. *Hello madam*, for example. Or, *How are you Dear?*

No, the messages that came from this phantom social account were real events in Betty's life, as far as Mabel could tell. And she *could* tell. That's what she'd spent the better part of the night before working on—cross-referencing dates and events.

She'd made it as far as the birth of her mother in 1961 by the time Mabel decided that the information was authentic.

After reading the rest and hesitantly accepting it all as truth, she wrote back to the sender. *Who is this?*

No response came. It never did. Not through the night and not that morning when Mabel, red-eyed from crying and losing a night's sleep, checked again. Her question hadn't even been seen yet, from all indications.

Now, as Mabel sat sipping truck-stop coffee and nibbling on an overcooked muffin, she opened her inbox to check for a reply.

Still, nothing.

A sigh escaped her lips in time for the waitress to return, bill clutched between her two fingers. She held it up, though, studying Mabel carefully, as if it was the wrong check. "You're not from around here, hey?"

"Sure, I am," Mabel protested. But she realized how she looked to other locals. She looked, well, different. In South Dakota or North, Mabel floated among a sea of blondes. Her hair, died darker than it was, stuck out for both its style and color but there were other things that set her apart. Her round eyeglasses. Freckles that she never once tried to hide. The way she dressed, too. Nothing about Mabel said midwestern girl. Instead, it was as if *Weirdo* was emblazoned across her chest. Her floral dress, something she'd made herself, on down to sensible, square-toe clogs. A disinterest in modern fashion in favor of a preference for crafting her own looks, from start to finish, was possibly to blame. In a big city, Mabel might pass for trendy or, at the very least, quirky. But here, she passed for just, plain odd. "I'm from Prairie Creek."

The waitress nodded slowly. "What brings you up this way?" Curiosity was clearly getting the better of this woman.

"I'm heading down from Fargo. I live there now, but I need to go home."

"Somebody die?" the woman asked, suspicion filling her work-worn features.

Mabel considered this question. Well, yes. There had been deaths. Was that why she was going home? Or was there another reason. The waitress grew bored, though, because she began to lower the ticket to the table just as Mabel muttered, "Yep. Something like that."

Chapter 6 — Griffin

Griffin spent the early hours of the next morning in the office with Dolores, the harried secretary left in the wake of Fletcher's abandonment. They were going through the paperwork Devery, the Realtor, had sent, and it was a lot.

The first order of business was to contact all board members, of which there were five. Fletcher made six, but he didn't count. Griffin's spot on the board was supposed to have happened with a new election, but that had gone out the window just as soon as Fletcher decided to sell.

"We've only got two to go," Dolores said on a sigh. They'd already phoned the first three, two of whom, Bob Merkle and Steve Hayfield, readily agreed to sign off on a sale. They were happy to placate Fletcher. They were his very best friends since the second grade, after all.

The third, Dick Knickerson, was out of town on

vacation and didn't believe in cell phones. According to his answering machine.

"Who's next?" Griffin asked wearily. He wanted out of there fast. There was no way he alone could purchase the company and take over, and the pain of all this was getting to him. He'd gone so far as to ask Logan if he wanted someone to head out to Minneapolis and take over for him in the contracting business Logan had started out there. Logan was open to it.

Dolores thumbed through their file folder. "Sue Gentry."

Logan looked over at the page and dialed her number. After several rings, she answered. "Hell-oo?"

"Hi, Mrs. Gentry, this is Griffin Dempsey with Dempsey and Son Logging Company." He cringed at the misnomer. "How are you today?"

Sue Gentry wasn't only a board member, she was also Miles' grandmother. "Oh, Griff!" she chirped pleasantly. "I heard! Oh, sweetie, I heard." Her voice was all waves of sadness and gushing commiseration.

"Oh," he replied, half deflated and half glad he wouldn't have to explain.

"I'm not one to judge, Griff, really I'm not. But how can Fletcher do this to you? Unless, was it your idea, sweetie?"

"No, Mrs. Gentry." He sighed again. "Dad and Tammy are heading down south for a while. He, um—it was his idea."

"Oh, my. Well, then—how do you feel about all of this, Griffin? Are you glad?"

"Ehh," he hemmed. "Umm," he hawed.

"Do I have a say? Is that why you're calling me?"

"We do need a vote, yes. Approval, basically. I mean, you'll be compensated for your shares in the company, and in order to move forward, we all have to sign off on the paperwork, the price, all that."

"What if I don't think we ought to sell?"

Griffin's heart paused momentarily. He hadn't considered the chance that they would simply not sell the company. He blinked and looked at Dolores who was gesturing wildly and mouthing *What! What?!*

"Mrs. Gentry, you're saying you'd vote against the sale?"

Dolores's eyes turned big. She was filled with the hope, clearly, that she still had a job.

Sue Gentry replied with a little laugh. "I'll vote whichever way you want me too, sweetie. It's not about us senior citizens. It's about young people. You're our future. We can be your voice."

For whatever reason, this point struck a chord with Griffin. Maybe because he was tired from a late night or maybe because his heart hurt from his dad's choice. He found himself mumbling a thank you and getting unnecessarily teary. After clearing his throat twice, he added, "And thank you, Mrs. Gentry. For what it's worth, even if we do sell."

"That's up to you, though. Isn't it, sweetie?"

"How so?" Griffin shrugged at Dolores who was following along best she could.

"Well you need a majority of the board to agree with the sale. If you don't have that, you'll be fighting an uphill battle. Or, should I say *Fletcher* will be fighting an uphill battle?"

"Right, but he can still sell. Just might not make the money he wanted. I think?" He was still a little foggy on all details related to selling the business. Having the board of directors added the complicated layer of seeking out approval and agreement and pay offs, all that.

"You've got one person right here who stands by the vice president of the company, firstly." She said this with an air of confidence, and Griffin's heart warmed.

"You mean me."

"Yes. I mean the future of logging. The person behind the scenes who cares not only for the company, but for our land here in the Dakotas. Our community. *Our future*. You sell this business, you don't know who might want a piece of the pie. It could get messy, and I don't only mean for Dempsey and Son. I mean for Prairie Creek. This business is a town staple. The people here deserve for it to go on in such a way that it benefits us. Right?"

"Right," Griffin agreed. "But, with all due respect, Mrs. Gentry, you're just one of the five board members. Two others have already voted to sell and to back my dad." As he said this, Griffin felt just as much a traitor to his own father as his father had been to him. Funny thing, working with family.

"And after me, you have two more. I can guess that Bob and Steve went the way of Fletcher. What about Dick?"

"He's on vacation."

"And Jim?"

Griffin referred to the print-out with the board members names, numbers, and addresses. Jim Kimble. He was the last one to call, and the one with whom Griffin was least comfortable speaking. "Mr. Kimble, yes. I—uh, I haven't called him yet. I figure he doesn't have much of a stake in the company anymore."

"Why? Because his wife died?" She clicked her tongue. "Sweetie, this is Logan's grandpa we're talking about. Have Logan take you over there. Talk to Jim. He's not mean, just sad. You get him, Dick, and me to say no, and that company, sweetie, it could be *yours*."

Chapter 7 — Mabel

When she arrived at Aunt Melba's cottage, no one was around. Maybe Mabel should have called ahead. She took for granted that her brother had said he was living there. Running the place as an inn. This was the problem with being out of touch with family. You lost track of them as easily as a sluggish old hound dog loses track of a housefly.

She parked anyway, committed now. To what, she wasn't sure. Mostly to figuring out who was sending messages from Grandma Betty's account. If she could figure it out, Mabel had a good feeling that maybe, just maybe, she could move on. She could marry Lucas and start a new chapter, for real.

Never without a project to keep her hands and mind busy, Mabel pulled out the yarn and hooks, turned the radio to the local country western station, and set about the first row of what she'd planned would become a generous lap blanket. Seashell patterned with pastel blue and butter yellow. She worked diligently but slowly, chain stitching over one hundred times, then single crochet, then big shell stitching into the next stitch, skipping three chains, single crochet again, then turning.

Mabel made her way clear through five radio commercials and twenty rows when the rumble of a truck engine rattled the Coke can in her cupholder. She twisted in her seat and saw a blue truck coming down the drive. There he was. Logan.

But he wasn't alone.

She packed her project back into her quilted bag, got out of her car, and wound her way to the front stoop, which she mounted. Hands on hips, she watched as Logan and an unknown female figure parked, got out and slowly made their way to her.

Mabel couldn't tear her eyes from the woman. She seemed familiar. It wasn't just her shock of red hair or height or beauty. Did Mabel know this person? Was she a cousin, maybe? No.

"Mabel," Logan's voice was strained. "What are you doing here?"

"Good to see you, too," Mabel snorted and folded her arms over her chest before landing an icy gaze on the ginger. "Hi." She tried for a nice voice and smile, but Mabel knew herself all too well. It came out, well, less than nice, probably.

The woman was unperturbed, however. She took a step closer to the porch and jutted out a long hand.

Freckles splashed up her arm, bringing her age down. "I'm Kelly. You must be Mabel."

So, they hadn't met. And yet, knowing this woman's name cemented the notion that she was distinctly, absolutely familiar to Mabel. The two shook hands and a slow warmth bloomed in Mabel's chest.

"How'd you know?" Mabel asked. Her attitude was dying off and so was the terseness in her tone and words.

"I've heard a lot about you from your brother." Kelly looked at Logan and smiled.

There was something in the smile that turned Mabel's stomach. Her budding smile fell away and she gave Logan a hard look. "Oh?"

"Mabel, you might recognize Kelly," he answered, appearing to pick his words with care. He looked at the redhead for some sort of permission. Kelly just smiled. "Kelly Watts," Logan added and shoved his hands as deep in his pockets as they'd fit. Mabel knew her brother's body language well. He was nervous for some reason. Was it Mabel? Or was it this woman?

Mabel narrowed her gaze back on Kelly. "Kelly Watts. I do know that name. Are you, did you go to high school with us?"

Kelly gave her a look of surprise. "No." She laughed.

Mabel felt foolish. "Sorry. Oh. I don't—I mean I do recognize you. I can't pin it down." She moved aside as the two joined her up on the porch and Logan's shoulders dropped. He relaxed enough to unlock the front door and let the two women in.

"I told you," Logan muttered.

Mabel whipped around and eyed her brother then Kelly. "Told her what?"

He looked insincerely sheepish. "That you didn't follow her."

Frowning, Mabel gave Kelly another good look up and down. "Follow her? What do you mean?"

"Mabel, Kelly is a famous social media influencer. Have you heard of Homestead and Hearth?"

The words triggered something in Mabel's brain. A magazine? Or a reality show? Blog? She nodded slowly. "That does ring a bell." She took Kelly in all over again. Understanding clicked into place. "Kelly Watts. Homestead and Hearth. Oh my gosh—you're like... you're like the next coming of Chip and Joanna. Pioneer Woman. Martha Stewart! I know you—you were in America Weekly. Like, recently." Bits and pieces of some story trickled into Mabel's head. She did know this woman. This woman was a famous person. Mabel wasn't usually impressed by things such as social media influencers, but being in the presence of one and having sort of *known* about this one...her jaw loosened and fell a few centimeters. "You're *Kelly Watts*."

Kelly laughed. "Yeah." Her eyes flicked down Mabel, like she was studying her sense of style. Kelly said, "I *love* that dress. Where did you get?"

"I made it." Then, Mabel shook her head. "I'm sorry, but what are you doing here?" Then she looked at Logan.

"Why is she here? How do you know her? Why didn't I know?"

"I tried to call you, like, a week ago, Mabel. But you never answer my calls."

Mabel's heart slowed. She had a hard time going even several minutes without her bad memories hitting her all over again. Logan's wife. Mabel's *friend*. Delilah. And of course, Grandma Betty. Often, Mabel wished she'd been Delilah, in the backseat without a belt on. Dead and oblivious to the pain left in the wake of one horrible car crash.

"You didn't answer my question," she murmured. Logan, though, gave her a look of exasperation. He pointed to the kitchen. "Come in. I'll make coffee."

The trio filed into Aunt Melba's kitchen, and Mabel took in the fact that it was exactly the same as it had always been. Logan hadn't changed a thing yet. Then, it occurred to her why Kelly Watts might be here. "Did he hire you?" she asked.

Kelly looked caught off guard and stammered for a moment before Logan answered for the both of them. "Yes. Yep. Kelly's here helping me do some restorations."

"Oh." Mabel's heart returned to its normal pace and she took her seat at the chair that faced the kitchen door. She had memories of being here at Aunt Melba's with Logan and their cousins, running around the farm, getting into trouble. Good memories. Memories that were overshadowed entirely by the bad one. "That's good," she managed at last.

"What are you doing here is the real question?" Logan brought fresh coffee over and filled three mugs that Kelly had put out. Kelly's familiarity with the kitchen might have struck Mabel as suspicious, if she weren't wrapped up in her drama.

"Right. Something weird is going on. I had to come figure out what it is. I...I, well..." She frowned and cleared her throat. "I just really need to know who is sending these." With that, she withdrew her phone, tapped the inbox, and flashed the screen to her brother, without even checking to see that a new message had come in.

Chapter 8 — Betty

J*anuary 1, 1970*

Diary—funny how I still call you by your name. I come to you today with a touch of hardness in my heart.

It's ten years since Jim and I have started our family. At nearly one child per two years, I have to confess: I'm tired. With our youngest, Wilhelmina, just turning a year, I have to wonder what's next for me?

Some days, I feel like I'm not in control of my life. Usually, it's Jim or one of the children whose demands come first. The children aren't easy, either. Nancy and Emily do their schoolwork and chores, but both are taking ballet lessons, and the cost is getting to be a lot for us. Even with the shop, which is stable.

John is signed up in baseball. Jim enjoys having that with him, but the laundry those two make! My! It's not only laundry, either. It's all the little things. Baseball pants get holes in the knees quick, so that takes patching. Then there's the Little League emblem what needs patching. And one of the other boys had his mother sew his last name onto his jersey. She must have stencils, because it came out perfect. Then John wanted his last name sewn on, and a handful of other boys whose mothers haven't got the time or fabric. As you can imagine, I was up late a few nights first making letter stencils then cutting, pinning, measuring, and sewing just about till my fingers bled.

I got it done, but something tells me there's more of that in my future!

Then there's the baby. Mina is challenging, and anyway, she gets the dregs of my energy, the poor thing. It's like she knows she's the last one and is stuck with hand-me-down clothes and toys. I also think she knows that whereas when she cries, I put her in her crib and close the door, but when Nancy cried as a baby, I held her and rocked her. Jim says we held all the others too much, and now we see what a baby ought to learn: to tough it out. Breaks my heart, but then what can I do? I've taken over the laundry part of the shop, and with three others plus Jim...

Jim is another matter. He's tired most days, and there isn't much left of him when I ask about the house. You see, in a two-bedroom apartment with growing children, we've run out of space. Mina is in a crib in our bedroom. Nancy and Emily share the second room. Poor John sleeps on a cot in the second room with the girls. It's not right he doesn't have a real bedroom. Soon enough, he'll be a little boy and not a toddler. Soon enough, Mina will be out of the crib, and then what?

I've asked Jim to find us a place in town. There are three-bedroom apartments at the building one street over. And then there's a lovely mobile home community south of town called Prairie Park. I hope one day we can find a place of our own there. Then Jim can use our current apartment as an office or, even better, maybe we can find a nice tenant. Then we'll have a little income to help with the slow times at the shop.

Well, I suppose I just sat down to complain, and that's what I've done. There's laundry to press. The baby is crying. I'd better go.

Yours,

Betty

Chapter 9 — Griffin

Griffin took Mrs. Gentry's advice just as soon as they finished their chat. But he didn't want to make it a text or another phone call. He figured he'd go down to the cottage, meet Logan in person, and, with any luck, convince him to drive to the town square where Old Man Kimble lived, in that little apartment upstairs of the old laundromat.

Dolores wished him luck and promised she'd keep working on Dick Knickerson in the mean time.

The drive to the cottage was a good ten minutes from Griffin's house in town, but he didn't mind the thinking time. He practiced what he'd say to his friend. How'd he convince Logan to help him convince his grandfather to help salvage the logging company. It would be a long shot. Everybody in town knew Old Man Kimble was of his own mind, unbending and strong willed to the bitter end.

By the time he arrived at the dusty drive that led up to Melba Ryerson's place, Griffin realized there was another vehicle there besides the blue Ford.

A white car. Griffin knew someone with a white car, but he was certain this couldn't be that same someone. Maybe Kelly Watts' assistant lady was back in town to collect her and drag her back to Texas and all that fame. Or maybe Logan had a real, live guest at the inn. Maybe he was doing well for himself. A ridiculous pang of envy crossed Griffin's chest, but he pushed it away and parked next to the truck, by the barn, before jogging up to the side of the house where the kitchen was, and where Griffin was used to entering.

He didn't knock on the window by the screen door in order to wait to be let in so much as to announce that he was coming in. That's how it had always been with Melba and surely would continue to be with Logan, country cottage inn or not.

After a quick rap, he pushed the button in on the old metal screen door and opened it, calling, "Logan, it's Griff!"

But Griffin got as far as one step onto the black-and-white laminate flooring and stopped dead in his tracks.

She looked entirely the same and totally different all at the same time. Her once chestnut hair was darker, nearly black. A sheet of it, cut even and short, sprayed over her forehead, covering up the creamy-smooth skin Griffin knew was under there. On her nose sat a pair of delicate silver glasses, round. She used to wear contacts.

Instead of a comfy sweatshirt and patch-kneed jeans, a sundress with little pink flowers all over it.

His eyes moved back to her face and settled for a moment on her lips, pale pink and pursed. She was even more beautiful than he remembered. "Mabel?"

Her green eyes blinked and her mouth fell open. "What are you doing here?" She looked around herself wildly, as if she were scared of him.

Griffin's instinct was to throw his hands up. "Sorry— I should have called ahead." But then he remembered why he was there. "Where's Logan?" It dawned on him the car in the drive was Mabel's. The same one from the accident just two years before. The same one she'd had in high school, longer ago still. How it had lasted college, moving cities, and a fatal car crash was nothing short of a miracle. Or a curse, maybe.

"He's—" she narrowed her eyes on him like she was seeing a ghost. Then, Mabel stood from the chair. Behind her, a second figure appeared. Another woman. Kelly Watts. Griffin flicked a brief glance up but his attention was sucked back to Mabel, who braced herself against the table as she took one tentative step in his direction.

Griffin's heart throbbed in his chest. His hands went slick. His mouth dry. "Why are you *here*?"

At his question, Mabel stopped moving forward, arrested, perhaps, by some far-off memory, some buried anger she'd clung to for so long that it lived in her bones. Behind Mabel, Kelly lifted her voice back into the bowels of the house. "Logan! Somebody's here!"

Logan appeared almost instantly. Griffin licked his lips then looked at his friend. "Hey. I—"

"Oh, crud." Logan knew better and was better able to articulate the general feel of that moment than anyone. *Oh, crud* was spot on. "Um, you two—um. Mabel's back, Griff."

Griff kept his eyes on Mabel who'd now retreated a step and crossed her arms over chest, partially turning to her brother and his girlfriend. The degree of awkwardness could not be understated. Did Mabel know about Kelly? Was she mad about that, too? Was she still legitimately mad at Griffin, or was this all just the aftereffects of a breakup gone so wrong that there was no way they could even acknowledge each other normally without the shadow of discomfort converging over them?

"I see that," Griffin replied to Logan's statement of obviousness. "How've you been, Mabel?" He tried for normalcy, but she wasn't going to have it.

"Great," she answered, her voice thick with sarcasm. "I'm *so* great. And you, Griffin? I heard you're selling the logging company. Big news for a small town, huh?" She smirked, but something different than scorn crossed her face. Indifference? He prayed not. The only thing worse than hating someone was feeling indifferent toward them, after all.

Griffin flashed a look at Logan. "Actually, that's why I'm here. I need to talk to Jim."

"Jim?" Mabel and Logan intoned this at the same instant, and their siblinghood, despite being as strained as it was, was recemented for all to witness. Griffin couldn't help but smile. When they were all younger, Mabel and Logan seemed to do that a lot, say the same thing at the same time. Almost like they'd been twins. That's just how close they were. *Were* being the operative verb.

"Jim Kimble."

"Grandpa Kimble?" they again said together. But no one was smiling now, and the brother and sister seemed almost annoyed to share the same thoughts in the same exact moments. Mabel pressed her lips in a line. "*You* need to talk to Grandpa Kimble? Why?" Her suspicion was so entirely visceral that Griffin knew there was something more to it.

But Griffin's request was innocent. "He's on our board of directors. I have to talk to him about selling." He looked guiltily at Logan. "I came here to see if you'd come with me."

When Griffin returned his stare to Mabel, it became clear that visiting Old Man Kimble might have to wait. Unless...

"I'll just take Logan along. And you'll never have to see me again, Mabel. You can stay here with Kelly. Your brother will be back in an hour. Two tops. Then, I'm out of your hair. Okay?" He knew just what she wanted to hear.

But he was wrong.

"That's where I'm going, though."

The room fell quiet and still. Clearly, her plans to

visit her grandfather were as much a surprise to Logan as they were to Griffin. The men exchanged a look.

"You are?" Logan scratched his head. Griffin watched Kelly pick up a mug of coffee from the counter and nurse it with mild interest from the background.

Griffin knew how women operated. They teamed up. Kelly wasn't only observing. She was there to defend Mabel, in all probability. But then—no. Surely they'd been arguing? Surely Mabel didn't accept that Kelly was fast becoming a serious romantic interest in Logan's life? Griffin found himself desperately interested to know what Mabel thought of Kelly. What she thought about her brother and Kelly. He desperately wanted to know, too, all about this fiancé of Mabel's. Lucas? What kind of a name was that, anyway?

"Yeah." Mabel's might dissipated under her brother's question. She sank back into her seat at the table and flicked a side glance at Griffin. He felt bad for just showing up. Maybe he should go. He could handle Jim Kimble on his own. He didn't really need Logan.

He started back for the door. "I'll leave. I don't want to interrupt what you have going on."

Mabel just gave him an icy look.

Logan stopped him, though. "Griffin, wait. Let's plan to go see Grandpa Kimble together. Maybe later? After Mabel makes her trip there? Would tomorrow be too late for you to talk to him?"

Griffin ran his hand up the back of his head then shook his hair out. "Ah. Well, it is urgent, I guess. But family first. You guys go. Whatever it is you need to do, go ahead. I'll touch base later." He backed out through the door.

Kelly pushed off from her slouching spot at the counter. "Logan, can I help? I could take Mabel there, to your grandfather's house, if you'd like?"

What happened next was nothing short of an explosion. It happened so fast and with such alarum, that Griffin had wished he had ducked out just a moment earlier.

The whole thing launched off because of one foolish action.

A kiss.

Chapter 10 —Mabel

J ust when Mabel was going to take Kelly up on her offer of accompaniment to Grandpa Kimble's, a shock descended over everything.

Logan said thank you to Kelly then, incredibly, he leaned over to her and gave her a peck on the cheek. A kiss.

A *kiss*. Logan kissed Kelly.

A scream materialized from the depths of Mabel's chest, but she wasn't a total whackjob. She contained it. She could not, however, contain the blood vessels bursting in her eyes. The throbbing pain in her chest. The confusion in her mind.

Nor could she contain her volatile propulsion from her seat to the farthest side of the kitchen—the door, where Griffin still lingered. "What!?" she yelled, once she was safely away from her brother, this stranger, and the cheek-peck. "What?" Mabel burned fire into Logan's eyes from where she stood. Her whole body felt hot and cold at once. It was ridiculous, probably. It was an overreaction, definitely. Logic, somewhere deep in the recesses of Mabel's brain, reminded her that they were all adults here. That Logan had a right to kiss who he wanted. And Kelly was beautiful. Why shouldn't he kiss her? But...but *Delilah*. It took every ounce of self-control for Mabel not to yell out, "What about your wife!"

Logan's wife was dead. Two years dead, in fact. A truth Mabel knew well. *All* too well.

Logan and Kelly froze in place. Kelly held a hand up to the cheek he'd kissed, almost as if Mabel had slapped it.

"Mabel, calm down." Logan took a step toward her, one hand outstretched, but the revulsion returned, and Mabel involuntarily backed right into Griffin. She didn't care. She held up both her palms to stop her brother.

"I am calm." She wasn't. "What's going on here?" Her pulse flickered in her neck, she could feel it. Heat rushed to her face. "With you two?" She kept her hands up, her back now felt the breeze of an open door. Griffin had passed through it and was holding it open for her.

Logan, who'd continued his forward movement, glanced back at Kelly, who still stood, stunned and hurt looking, at the counter. Mabel fully expected him to say that *nothing* was going on. Nothing *should* be going on between her brother and anyone, least of all some B-list celebrity who was camping out in South Dakota for Heaven knows what reason.

He did not, however, say that *nothing* was going on. He went in the opposite direction. "Kelly and I are dating."

Mabel felt sick. Images of Delilah flashed in her mind. Then, images of Logan, smiling and happy and holding someone who was not his wife. Mabel whipped around, her gaze landing on Griffin. A poor excuse for a last resort, but, well, that's what last resorts were, weren't they? "Take me with you," she demanded breathlessly. Then, "Please," on a whisper.

Griffin threw an apologetic look to Logan, then wrapped an arm around Mabel and swept her off to his own truck, a red Chevy.

A new one. Different than the truck he'd had the last time she'd seen him.

And then, Mabel allowed a small thought to cross her wounded, writhing mind. *What else was new in Prairie Creek?*

Chapter 11 — Betty

M
arch 21, 1975

Diary, I've been terribly absent in my writing to you. You might expect me to say that a lot has happened!

I'll disappoint you, instead. In truth, not a lot has happened, despite how busy these past years have been. And nothing terribly important, just the day-to-day business of life as a mother and a wife. Oh, and a laundress.

I talked to my own mother just this past Sunday. We had a chance to sit and chat like old friends. It was nice. Nancy and Emily watched John and Mina for me so I could have a "break." My mother said when we were growing up, having children meant you had <u>help</u>. That struck me as funny, since having children means I NEED

ELIZABETH BROMKE

help! Ha-ha! They are a wonder, though. There is nothing I'd rather do than raise my babies. Jim agrees. He loves the kids.

By the way, did I ever mention we found a new home? Yes. In '73, Jim surprised me with a special trip north of town to a little neighborhood. A real one, with real houses, wood and brick sort of like in "The Three Little Pigs." He blindfolded me with a red kerchief and after he guided me out of the car and up a little walkway, he pulled the kerchief away and there it was. A beautiful home, red bricks ran around the bottom half with white-painted wood trim on the top half. Something out of a fairy tale, to be sure.

It was my birthday and Christmas gift all wrapped into one, and gee! I felt pretty fancy. I still do, even two years on. We have three whole bedrooms plus a "den." The girls have their own room. John has his. Jim and I have ours—and did you know we upgraded to one of those King-size beds?

Anyhow, Jim keeps a roll-top desk in the den so that he can do his financials at night. That's not all. Jim dedicated half of the den to my sewing. In there, not only do I have a real, live sewing desk (Jim made it for me this past Easter!) and my Singer, but I also have a shelf for all my crafting and sewing supplies. Tins for the thread. Bins for the yarn and fabric. And my own little sewing box that Mother gave me for my wedding shower. Remember? I told you about it. The mustard-yellow one. It fits almost all my doodads, as Jim calls them. Then, in a separate little

54

shoebox I keep old lightbulbs for darning socks. Any sock that springs a hole, I put it in a second shoebox, then on Sundays, I spend an hour or two after church working on the socks or whatever else needs a darn or a patch. I'm not sure I'm ever happier than when I'm in my sewing room. I mean, the den.

Our kitchen is perfect. A great big table fits all of us right there, inside the kitchen itself. Then there's the living room with our television set, a sofa and two easy chairs. Jim loves the easy chairs. (I secretly love them, too).

Life is perfect.

Oh, and? Here is the biggest news for the Kimble family...

Nancy has a boyfriend.

Gee!

Jim thinks she's too young to date, so it's a bit of a mother-daughter secret. You won't tell, will you?

His name is Norman Ryerson. Yes, you guessed it. My best friend's son! I know this is far, far off, but if they end up getting serious, do you think I should give the boy my wedding ring for his proposal? Okay, I've gone too far!

Chapter 12 — Griffin

Griffin was stunned. Stunned as he led Mabel into his truck, where he opened the door, helped her up, closed the door, rounded the back, and jumped in on his side.

Mabel Ryerson, his high school sweetheart and officially the one who got away, was retreating to his arms. Some twenty-odd years after the last time he'd ever actually spoken with her. They'd each lived another life in that span of time. They'd kissed other people. Developed other secrets, too, probably. Or maybe not. Griffin only truly had the one secret in his heart. The one that had ruined everything.

It took him a moment to mentally situate himself before he started the engine.

Mabel must have taken the same moment, because she was covering her face with her hands. Almost like a little girl. "Hey," he whispered. "It's okay."

She shook her head behind her hands but then pulled them down and whipped around back towards the cottage.

Griffin followed her search, but there was no sign of Logan or Kelly. They weren't in pursuit. Not yet, anyway.

"Where to?" Griffin tried for casual, but his hands were clammy on the steering wheel. He tried to focus on the next thing. Driving.

Mabel didn't answer immediately, so he let her be and started the engine and rolled out of the property slowly.

Once they got to the roadway, Griffin turned left. It was the only sensible way to go, back towards town. They could grab a bite at the café or go for a drive, but they'd better turn left to do either one.

When Mabel still hadn't said anything by the time he'd hit the highway, Griffin finally looked over at her.

She stared straight ahead, but he could see tears streaming down her face, glistening against her creamy, pale skin.

"Mabel? You okay?" Griffin shifted uncomfortably and applied his foot to the gas. The truck roared up to speed, and he made the executive decision to head into town. They didn't have to stop anywhere. They could just coast down Main and come out again on the highway. Ultimately, he figured she'd want to go back to the cottage.

Maybe.

Mabel sniffed. "Not really."

His heart sank. Of course she wasn't okay. He knew why, too. It was easy enough to figure. "You came back and your brother suddenly has a girlfriend. That's gotta sting." He said this all very plainly. Nothing dramatic about it. Just the facts.

Mabel sniffed again. "I had no idea he was ever going to date again."

"Yeah." Griffin kept his eyes on the road. He wanted to ask her why she *had* come home, but that wasn't important now. What was important was making sure Mabel was okay. And also talking to Old Man Kimble, still... He considered carrying on with that particular errand. But, no.

Her sniffles had dried out, and when Griffin turned to Mabel, he saw she looked, well, like herself again. Just with darker hair and those cute bangs. Griffin had never once seen a set of bangs he could appreciate. Until now. He couldn't help it. A small smile fought its way up from his heart to his lips. Mabel pulled something out of her purse. A clump of yarn, it looked like. And a metal or aluminum needle that looked to be about a thousand times the size of a sewing needle.

"You're still knitting?" Griffin remembered in high school how Mabel's favorite pastime was to do little crafty projects, like sew curtains and aprons and sometimes woolen scarves, too.

"It's crochet."

"What's the difference?" He was only trying to make conversation.

"The difference is," she said pointedly, "I don't have to listen to the clinking of knitting needles when I crochet. It's just this hook." She pulled the silver stick from the yarn and wiggled it for his benefit.

"Oh yeah. I know what you're talking about. My mom used to knit. I kind of liked the noise."

Mabel returned the hook to her yarn and pushed it through. "Well, I *don't*," she replied acerbically.

"Okay," Griffin said, confused about her sudden shift. "Sorry?"

Mabel glanced his way and shook her head. "It's fine. It's...just, after the accident, I have a hard time with sharp noises. Even knitting needles. That's all." She was stoic about it, but Griffin's heart sank.

"Oh, Maby," he murmured, using a nickname he hadn't uttered since high school graduation. "I'm sorry."

"Really, it's fine. Just one of those things!" She said this brightly and pushed ahead. "So, you need to see my grandpa? About your dad's company?"

Griffin let out a sigh. He'd let her talk about the accident when she was ready. Clearly, she wasn't. Not yet, anyway. "I really do need to talk to Mr. Kimble. And today, if possible." Something occurred to him. "You came home to see him, too?"

"Not exactly." Her mouth remained a thin line, but she was talking to him, and that was something.

"Does your visit back have to do with, um—" he cleared his throat "—your engagement?" Griffin lifted a curious eyebrow at her, and clear as day, Mabel's cheeks reddened. "I'm sorry. That's seriously not my business. Not by a mile."

"No. It has nothing to do with that." A beat. Then, "Anyway, how'd you know?"

"It's Prairie Creek. Word gets around. Plus, I mean, obviously I'm still friends with your brother even if you and I aren't—" What *weren't* they, anyway? Dating anymore? Obviously. It had been literally two decades since they dated.

"Aren't what?"

Griffin looked at her. Her mouth had curled up on one side. Her eyes, dry now, glimmered playfully behind her glasses. Was she...*flirting*?

No way.

He shifted again in his seat and got ready to take the turn off into town. "Aren't on speaking terms, I figure," he replied at length.

"Well, here we are," she replied. "Speaking."

Griffin turned onto Main Street. He figured they could at least drive to the town square, and from there decide where to go next, be it Jim Kimble's or somewhere else. "True," he replied. "Anyway."

"Anyway." Mabel's tone had lightened considerably since they'd left the cottage.

Griffin said, "So, you're not back for wedding planning."

Mabel laughed. "I'm not getting married here."

"Oh. Right." He felt itchy. "You're not back to meet Kelly, either, I guess."

"Ha!" This didn't come out as a laugh but instead as a snort. "I didn't know she'd be there. I didn't know anyone would be there and least of all some...*hook up*." Her voice drifted back down to a level of disgust reserved for, well, disgusting things. Griffin had to confess, though, despite understanding why Mabel was upset, he wasn't disgusted with Logan and Kelly's blossoming relationship. He was happy for them. So, sue him.

"So, why are you back, Mabel?" he kept his voice soft and low. He liked this. Their conversation. He wanted to keep it going. He wanted her to stay in his truck with him or come with him to Jim Kimble's house or whatever. "Why do you need to see your grandpa?"

They'd arrived at the laundromat storefront, and Griffin put the truck in park, but he didn't shut off the engine.

Mabel let out a sigh, tucked her yarn and hook into her bag, and unfastened her seatbelt. But instead of getting out, she pulled her phone from the bag, tapped around for a minute, then flashed the screen his way so he could read it.

Chapter 13—Mabel

It was a risk: Bringing Griffin into her fold like this.

Not only a risk in that Griffin had no right to her innermost struggles, but a risk in that if Lucas knew...he'd flip out.

And she wouldn't blame him.

Sometimes, though, you just had to do whatever the next logical thing to do was. And if she had decided to stick to Griffin over Logan, then she might as well spill the beans. After sharing with Griffin that she'd received messages containing Grandma Betty's diary entries, he made an important point.

"You think your grandfather sent the messages?"

Mabel considered this. "Honestly, no. He doesn't have a computer, I'm pretty sure. I don't think his phone even gets internet. I could be wrong, but it makes no sense."

"But that's why you wanted to come see him? To tell him about this or ask about who could be sending your grandmother's diary entries?"

"I figure he knows who would have her diary, if it's not him."

"And what if it is him who has the diary?" Griffin asked. "But he didn't send the messages?"

Mabel frowned. "If he doesn't have the diary and didn't send the messages, well, that would be creepy."

"You think he can handle it?"

"Handle what? You asking him to steamroll your dad's liquidation plan?" she smirked, flicked through to another interface on her phone and showed him a text exchange between her and Lucy Gentry. Was he really too dense to not consider the inevitable? Mabel and her bestie had conspired. Mabel knew all about Griffin's drama.

"Ah, you don't talk to your family, but you talk to Lucy." A thought looked to pass behind his eyes. "Lucy, your best friend. Lucas, your fiancé. That's quite the coincidence. Do you ever get the two confused?"

"Are we talking about my engagement or your chance at winning over my grandfather?"

"We were talking about your grandmother's haunted messages, actually."

Mabel set her jaw and folded her hands over her chest. If she was going to be forced to carry on conversation with her high school sweetheart, the one who crashed her world, who swept her up in the grandeur of young love only to squash it all with one fell swoop, then Mabel was going to go hard on him. She ignored his point, because Mabel knew that no matter what they talked about, there was the thing they *weren't* talking about.

Them.

Sure, Griffin cared about himself. He cared about his career. But he did not care about her. Or about *them.* Whatever they were or used to be. She went on. "Anyway, speaking of engagement and Luc*as,* I need to make a call." She gave Griffin a phony smile and let herself out the truck before wandering to the bench outside of Grandpa Kimble's shop.

Then, Mabel finally called her fiancé back.

Lucas answered on the first ring. "I've been worried sick, Mabel. Where are you? Are you okay?"

She lowered her voice and her head. "Hi. I'm sorry. I'm fine. I'm in Prairie Creek. I sent you a text this morning. Did you not get it?"

"I did, and when I replied, you never answered—"

Mabel couldn't hear him well. "Lucas, can you talk louder? We have a bad connection or something."

Lucas raised his voice to the point that Mabel had to hold the phone a short distance from her ear, but she let him talk.

"I can't believe you went there, Mabel. *Again*. Wasn't the funeral enough?" He was referring to Melba's service just weeks earlier. The one he'd attended, too, acting more like her bodyguard than her boyfriend.

Mabel raised her voice a little, too, though not to the strength of Lucas's. She had to convince him that she'd made a good choice. "It's the messages. What I told you last night. I have to find out, Lucas. I can't explain it other than I have to close this chapter. I have to find out where they're coming from. Maybe it will...I don't know help me heal?" She hated that she was suggesting that there was any way she *could* heal.

"You can find out by making phone calls. Running off on a last-minute road trip isn't safe, Mabel. Or smart. And your family—I'm not there to protect you."

A sound came from behind Mabel, and she whipped around to see Griffin standing too close, his head cocked. He mouthed, *Protect you from what?*

She hissed at Griffin, "You're listening?"

Griffin's hands shot up, and he fell back a step. "I'm sorry!" he said.

Lucas asked, "Who's sorry? Who's with you, Mabel? Is it Logan?"

"No," she assured him. But it was the wrong assurance.

"Then who is it, Mabel? Is it—is it *him*?" Mabel cringed at Lucas's question. The flagrant rage in his voice was warranted. She was a fool.

Should she lie? Hang up on Lucas? Tell the truth and accept his wrath? The best option was to avoid the question all together. "Lucas, I have to go. I'm here at Grandpa's shop. I'm going in. I'll call you later."

"Mabel, is it *him*?" Lucas repeated through clenched teeth, but Mabel didn't really care. She ended the call and looked at Griffin. "Thanks for that."

"For what? You're not allowed to be around me?"

"Let me put it to you this way, if you were engaged, how would your fiancée feel if you were spending time with me?"

"Are we spending time together? Is that what this is?" he asked.

Mabel pursed her lips. "Not by choice, and that's what Lucas won't understand." Mabel started for the buzzer that her grandfather had installed when he'd moved back into the shop and converted it to his home.

"So you just hang up on him, then."

She turned back and gave Griffin a hard look. "You don't get to do that."

"Do what?"

"Tell me how to live my life. You had your chance. You lost it."

He was unaffected, because he followed her right up to the buzzer. Mabel was reminded just how confrontational Griffin could be, and it irritated her. "You haven't changed, Mabel."

"Sure, I have. I got a haircut. I stopped sewing. I'm marrying someone else?" Her voice hitched up on that last note to rub it in. "I'm older now and wiser."

"You're the same." He went as far as to poke her in the arm with his finger, and this really got her riled up.

Mabel fumed and pushed the buzzer then decided she'd have to now ignore Griffin. She'd have to just get this over with then get home and deal with Lucas. *Ugh*. A headache was coming on.

Griffin, in typical Griffin form, wasn't quick to give up. "You don't like to face the hard stuff. You didn't tell your fiancé that yes, you're with *Griffin*. Your ex. And why? Because he, what? He's jealous?"

"I didn't tell him, because I actually *am* facing something hard. I'm facing my past. My grandmother's death and now her messages and her widower. So, actually, I *have* changed, like I said." She sounded like a teenage brat, but she didn't care. Mabel wasn't here to see or talk to Griffin. He was shrapnel to her visit and mission. Irrelevant maiming that she'd survive even if it slowed her down.

"If I were him, I'd be jealous." Griffin wouldn't quit.

She buzzed again then squinted up at him. "What are you even talking about, Griff?" She meant to say Griffin. She hated that she'd said Griff. She hated that he still had his sexy long hair and that his face was the same and his jaw was sharper and his eyes were greener and—she hated that'd she'd come home. Lucas was right.

"I'm just saying," Griffin replied, "if I were Lucas, and I knew about *me*—knew about *us* and what we had, I'd be so jealous I'd drive down here myself. I wouldn't let you spend a single moment with me."

"Oh, so you think I'm not trustworthy." She felt her skin tingling. Her neck was probably flushed. She felt hot. And weird. And like she could hardly breathe. Griffin stepped closer to her, closing their gap as he lowered his head nearer to her face.

"I think you still love me."

Glass shattered behind them.

Chapter 14 — Griffin

Griffin knew he was pushing his luck. That's why, when Mabel whipped around to the muted sound of something breaking inside of the shop, he fell back a step. Being with her was like falling into a trance. Like he couldn't control his pulse, his breaths. Everything went fast and slow at once, and Mabel was engaged now. He'd better knock it off.

Anyway, it wasn't Griffin's style to push boundaries. Sure, he didn't mind a little confrontation. A little mischief. But he wasn't about to cross the line.

Mabel's hands covered her ears and she winced.

Pressing a gentle hand to Mabel's lower back as a way to comfort her, Griffin then stepped up to the window and tried to peek through the curtains that covered it. "He's okay," Griffin assured her. "Just looks like he knocked something over." He glanced back at Mabel. "Are you okay?"

"I'm okay." She nodded and gave him a grateful smile.

Griffin tried for the door, but it was still locked. Another peek through the curtains showed that Old Man Kimble was moving slowly past a broken lamp and toward the door. "It's a lamp. It looks like he just knocked over a lamp." Griffin turned back to see Mabel still had her hands over her ears, and now her eyes were closed. "Mabel, it's okay." He moved to her, and it occurred to Griffin, then, that this was more than the noise from within. There was something else there, deeper, that seemed to startle her. Well, she was beyond startled. She looked—traumatized.

Before he could do more to soothe her, the curtains swept aside, and the glass door opened outward. The smell of something familiar blasted him in the face. It reminded Griffin of his own grandparents. A little bit moth ball, a little bit musty fabric—a lot of warm memories. "Mr. Kimble," Griffin started, finding the right re-introduction of himself in the presence of a clearly upset Mabel, the man's granddaughter. "It's me, Griffin Dempsey. Fletcher's son?"

Old Man Kimble scowled at him. "Fletcher. All right." Then, his drooping eyes crawled to Mabel. He didn't say it, but Griffin knew that the man was taken aback at the sight of his granddaughter. Griffin had better grease the wheels on the reunion.

"I've brought your granddaughter here. Mabel. She's

in town to visit you." Even if it wasn't exactly the truth, Griffin knew it was the right thing to say.

"Mabel?" Old Man Kimble perked up and shuffled forward through the door. "Mabel?"

Mabel pulled her hands down from her ears, finally, and looked up. Her face lifted. "Hi Grandpa." She smiled at him and without another moment's hesitation stepped into an embrace. Her distress melted away, and it was clear that Mabel needed this.

Griffin envied the pair. He'd always wanted that sort of relationship with *anyone* in his family. Even his own mother, who was a kind enough woman, had her own thing going. If Griffin were to stop in to say hello to Sheena Dempsey, he'd be met with *I'm in the office, Griff! Be out soon!* Only to leave him waiting half an hour until she re-emerged, her work headset on. She'd be done up for the day and a done-up woman, to Griff, was unapproachable. Even if it was his own mother. He preferred simplicity.

"Come on in, you two," Old Man Kimble shuffled back through the door with Mabel holding his hand. Griffin followed them into the stuffy downstairs space.

Once inside, it was a marvel. The shop hadn't changed since they were kids, Griffin and Mabel. She must have seen it more recently than he, but even Mabel appeared to wonder at it all.

To the left, there was the front desk. A yellow-orange Formica counter faced a row of brown, vinyl-backed chairs with metal frames. Behind the counter was the cash register, which happened to be a seriously vintage till. Truly an antique, no doubt. They weren't entirely uncommon in Prairie Creek, where people preferred to enact maintenance on things like appliances and machinery as opposed to upgrading to the newest technology.

Beyond the counter and till was a metal rod hanging horizontally. Lined up along it were wire hangers, papered over. *Kimble's Sew 'n' Vac.* Beyond that, although it was harder to see from just the entryway, was the little sewing room where Mrs. Ryerson had taken up Grandma Betty's work so many years ago. With a mother like Sheena, who didn't sew, and a father like Fletcher, who didn't subscribe to shopping, Griffin had brought in pieces of clothing once or twice for Mrs. Ryerson to do up. The suit he'd bought for prom, taken in. A pair of slacks for his first job interview, taken in. That sort of thing.

Griffin remembered the last time he was there, hanging around waiting for Mabel to get off her shift so he could take her down the street for root beer floats.

He shook the memory and followed Old Man Kimble and Mabel past the bank of washing machines and the wall of dryers to a tucked-away staircase.

"Grandpa, let me help you." Mabel danced awkwardly beside the old man, trying to find the right position to provide support.

Griffin asserted himself. "Here," he said, and took Mr. Kimble's arm and hooked it through his then led the way up, after Mabel who'd squeezed ahead to open the door at the top of the stairs.

Forcing his eyes on the steps just ahead of them so he wouldn't be tempted to look at his ex-girlfriend's butt, Griffin started practicing his proposition to Jim Kimble, should he have the chance to give it.

Mr. Kimble, I understand you're a vocal board member still, and I want to implore you to consider what a sale of the business and its liquid assets could mean. Not just for the company or for me, but for the town. Think of the change, and I'm not one to rail against change, but we can agree, I'm sure that my father's decision to sell could mean something big.

What *could* it mean? Griffin could kick himself for not better preparing after having gotten the green light from Susan Gentry.

Once they were inside of the little apartment on the second floor, Griffin felt as though he were entering the second dimension of this time warp. The apartment was straight out of an episode of *I Love Lucy*. There were touches of Aunt Melba's cottage, like with the sink and faucet and the laminate flooring. But there were other aspects that contradicted the country setting, opting for something that might have passed for an attempt at metropolitan back in the fifties or sixties. A green velveteen sofa. Two maroon easy chairs. A box TV complete with bunny ear antennae. A wood laminate veneer table and four art deco-style chairs were curled up in a small nook of the living room, he saw as they followed Mr. Kimble through the narrow, galley kitchen and into a back bedroom. A braided rug in green and orange ran down white laminate flooring. Crammed between a very old Frigidaire and a white oven were mounted black-painted cabinets with red trim. Nothing matched, and yet everything matched.

In the room where Mr. Kimble had led them, a similar design scheme existed. It must have once been a bedroom, according to its shape, but now there was a lone easy chair, blue velveteen. It sat in the center of the room and next to it was a folding TV tray, brown laminate, and brass metal legs. Atop of that a single, neatly re-folded newspaper. Atop of the newspaper, a crossword, a magnifying glass, and a felt-tip pen. A drink, maybe a highball, had recently been finished and rested on a square of fabric.

Mr. Kimble also had a rolltop desk that reminded Griffin of something Ebenezer Scrooge might sit at. Tucked into the middle of the desk was a wood-backed desk chair with wheels and a brown, fabric seat.

On the other side of the room it looked like a different world. Lighter colors, pastels, yellows, came together in what must have been a memorial to Mrs. Kimble's—Betty's—sewing space. It was all very simple, neat, and minimal. Staged, even, as though Mr. Kimble had hauled a sewing room into this room and set it up to look like she was still using it.

A sewing table with a machine sat centrally to the area. A small wooden chair. A rack, maybe to dry out smaller laundry items, delicates like pantyhose. A shallow, tall shelf. At the top of the shelf, was a row of very small knickknack-looking things, all matching and metallic. Clearly, a collection of them, orderly and precious. The little scene made Griffin's heart hurt for Mabel. For Mr. Kimble, too.

Mabel looked wholly uncomfortable to be in the room. Griffin watched as she purposefully turned her back on Betty's corner, knelt beside her grandfather who had eased into the blue chair, and took control of the conversation. "Grandpa," she started carefully, slowly, with a quick look at Griffin. "Do you remember how Grandma kept a diary? A journal?"

Jim, who looked comfortable enough but was still catching his breath from the downstairs adventure, either didn't hear her or was giving ample chance for his memory to find that particular bit of history of his wife's life.

After several moments wherein Jim sat breathing heavily and staring at the silenced console television with a baseball game playing on it, Mabel looked more meaningfully at Griffin.

He took his cue. "Mr. Kimble," he spoke loudly, "Mabel wants to know if you recall a book that Betty had?"

"A book?" he looked at Griffin, befuddlement playing out over his mouth and behind his thick glasses. "Which?"

"It was her diary," Griffin said, again, loudly. Mabel

looked at him gratefully and edged closer to her grandfather.

"Grandpa, do you remember? Grandma kept a diary? A journal?" She'd raised her voice too and slipped her hands around her grandfather's. "She wrote in it sometimes," Mabel added.

Old Man Kimble was unmoved by the question, and yet he nodded. His eyes remained on the television, but he said, "Yes. I have it!" he spoke loudly, too.

"You do?" Mabel's eyes lit up. "Where is it?"

Jim leaned into Griffin. "I've got it there in the living room! It's with my telephone!"

Griffin looked for Mabel's approval to retrieve the book. She nodded.

He found it easily, on the laminate-top kitchen table that was just around the wall of the living room. The journal sat innocuously beneath a cell phone that was plugged into the wall. Griffin slid the journal out from under the phone and carried it back to the living room. "Here you go, Mr. Kimble!" He held the book out for Jim to see, but Jim just pointed to Mabel.

"Did you get it?" he asked Mabel.

She took the book from Griffin and answered, "Yes. Thank you. It's right here." Was he going blind? Possibly. Griffin felt for the guy.

Mr. Kimble frowned and shook his head. "No. I mean, did you get the messages, Mabel?"

Chapter 15 — Betty

S eptember 15, 1980

Well, times sure are changing. All of the children are in school now, which you know. My entries of late have been tediously dull, but it is a joy to look back and see Emily's last dance rehearsal here and John's baseball championship win there. Ah. The life of a family. So small but so full of life.

One big event that has happened is in fact a series of big events. And it all just happened this past weekend, so you can be sure that you, Diary, are getting the latest breaking news, as they say.

First things, my Nancy has gotten married. Yes, to Norman. They call him Norm. You know how I feel about nicknames. So critical—well, did you know that Norm calls Nancy "Nance?" I just love it. Norm and Nance. I think they were meant to be.

I'm not sure if I entered this detail in an earlier entry, since I've been just so busy! But I feel it important to share on the off-chance I have a granddaughter one day and she wants to read this. I made Nancy's wedding dress. Can you believe that? It sounds unbelievable, I know. But I did it. Gladys helped. I'd never worked with satin or chiffon before, but Gladys had, I guess. I have experience with lace, so we pulled off a miracle. White tulle for the underskirt, then a white chiffon slip. The dress itself was satin, and I made a lace overlay. It was a lot of work, delicate work. Nancy looked stunning. The long sleeves enhanced her sinewy arms, and the full skirts were so shapely. Nancy felt it was a little old-fashioned, but in the end, all three of us agreed she was a classic bride. Beautiful, white as the fresh-fallen snow, and ready to begin the rest of her life. I'll forever cherish the memory of making that dress and watching my eldest daughter walk down the aisle in it. A mother's dream, to be sure.

I'm on cloud nine, right now, Diary!

But that's not all I have to share.

With the wedding, came another big change in the Kimble-Ryerson family, Diary.

I'm going back to work.

You read that right, Diary! No more Mrs. Kimble.

Okay, well, I'm still Mrs. Kimble, but now there'll be a little more to me. Jim has given me permission to open a *small mending and tailoring operation out of the back of the shop. That's not all, Diary. Guess who'll be my first employee?*

You guessed it.

Nancy.

Oh, did you think my late breaking news stopped there?

No, siree. Diary. In a way, life is just beginning. At least, for the newest member of the Kimble-Ryerson clan, it is!

That's right. Nancy is pregnant. She has a feeling it's a boy. If so, I just know he's going to be the sweetest, most kind-hearted little man in the world. Maybe I'll go find a pattern for baby bibs...

Chapter 16 — Mabel

"Yes, Grandpa, I got the messages." she replied earnestly. It was unbelievable to her that Grandpa Kimble had not only found her grandmother's diary, had not only *transcribed* it into type, but had also managed to upload the entries online, find Mabel, and send them. Successfully. That didn't even include the fact that he'd have had to create a profile for his dead wife. Not that the profile was filled out to any degree, but still.

She had so many questions. Before she could ask even one, the downstairs buzzer blared near the apartment door. "Someone's here," Griffin pointed out the obvious.

Grandpa Kimble waved it off. "They've got a key. It's just a formality."

Who had a key? Two years had gone by, and a lot had happened, apparently. So much for fading into oblivion when he got to be old. Grandpa Kimble was a mover and a shaker.

Mabel felt pressed by time: the time crunch to get back home and make things right with Lucas. The window of time she had to spend with her grandfather.

And with Griffin Dempsey.

"Grandpa, did Grandma Betty always have a Facebook account?"

The old man frowned deeply. "She always did!" he answered with a haughtiness to suggest Mabel's grandparents were far more technologically savvy than she'd ever realized. But if Betty Kimble had always had a Facebook—always being a relative term to the birth and evolution of the platform—then how come Mabel had never known about it?

She pulled her phone from her bag and tapped into the app. That's when she saw it. A friend request she'd overlooked or missed because she was never on Facebook. A friend request from Betty Kimble, dated back exactly three years. Mabel could kick herself for not being a better steward of her apps. Who knew what it might have meant had Mabel accepted the friend request when it came through? Maybe it was one of those things, like the butterfly effect. It could have reversed the course of history. It could have saved everyone.

Mabel gave her brain a shake. She was being ridiculous. She turned her attention back to Grandpa. "Okay, so you found her diary and decided you wanted it to be online? Is that what happened?"

He coughed. "No. I did what Betty wanted is all."

What did Grandma want?

A knock came at the door.

Griffin stood up. "Should I get that?"

Grandpa waved Griffin off now just as he had the buzzer. This was not a man who made a Facebook profile, typed up pages and pages of diary entries, found his estranged granddaughter—they hadn't addressed that matter, by the way—and then connected all the dots. It made no sense. Then there was the *why* behind it all. "Grandpa, was there a reason you meant to send me her diary entries? Was there something I needed to know?"

"For starters, you should know that it was me."

Mabel's head snapped up to the source of the response. At the door, passing by Griffin, were Logan and Kelly, together. Mabel could hardly see them as the couple they apparently were, but if it was true—if her brother was legitimately dating Kelly Watts—well, they looked good together.

"What was you?" she answered Logan, releasing Grandpa Jim's hand and standing to face her brother. Mabel shot a look at Griffin, but he only shrugged.

"Maybe you three could go into the living room to chat? I'll hang here with Grandpa Jim," Griffin suggested to Mabel, Logan, and Kelly as if Grandpa Kimble was out of the equation already.

Logan agreed immediately. "I think that's a good idea."

"So, Grandpa Jim had nothing to do with the messages? He just asked me if I got them," Mabel pointed out. Grandpa was not out of the equation. He *was* the equation.

"He had everything to do with the messages," Logan replied. "But—"

There was no but. They could clear the air now. As a big, happy family. After all, if Logan was going to play house, then he'd better do it right. "We can discuss it here. With Grandpa. And you," she pinned a look on Kelly.

Mabel dropped back to her knees and collected the old man's frail hand again. It felt good to be with her grandfather. It felt like something that had died in Mabel was budding back to life in a small way. Her ancestry. Her familial ties.

Then, there was Logan. And Kelly. Mabel did her best to contain the scowl she wanted to flash the woman.

For her part, Kelly appeared as nervous and uncomfortable as anyone would in this situation. She even said, "Should I go, Logan?"

"No. You're part of this, too."

"What do you mean *she's* part of this."

"I don't have a Facebook. I don't know how it works!" Logan raised his voice freely.

"What does that have to do with *anything*?" Mabel was beyond confused. She looked at Griffin for help, but he was none, of course.

Well, he was *some*. "Let's just everyone take a deep breath."

"Shut up, Griff," Logan growled.

"He's right." Kelly held up a hand. Her freckles belied her age, which Mabel knew from a quick Google search. She wasn't older than Logan like Mabel had suspected. She was exactly his age in fact. For whatever reason, this annoyed Mabel even more. Kelly said, "Griffin is right. Let's slow down." The redhead tucked a strand of her hair behind her ear and lowered to the ground adjacent to Mabel. She crossed her legs, and the sheer length of them made for a silly sight, and Mabel wanted to laugh, but she also wanted to cry. For a million reasons.

Mabel wanted to cry for seeing Griffin again and knowing that she couldn't have him, not like she had Lucas. She wanted to cry over Grandma Betty's and Delilah's deaths all over again. She wanted to cry about seeing Grandpa Jim and the fact that they had hardly said hello before Mabel started in on her great, big, last-minute mission. She wanted to cry about the fact that her brother had found a place to contain his grief so well that it didn't rule his life anymore. Unlike Mabel's grief, which was wild and dominated just about everything. Every decision she made.

Mabel wanted to cry that she had to leave Prairie Creek again soon. She'd have her answers shortly, then it'd be home to her receptionist job and her sterile condo and her regimen of pills and home to Lucas. Tears pricked at the corner of her eyes, but instead of wiping them away, she let them sit. Maybe if Mabel kept letting herself be sad, she'd get it over with. Maybe she could stop running and start dealing. Maybe that's why she'd come home after all.

Chapter 17 — Griffin

Griffin needed to leave. It was time. He had no business being a part of a Ryerson-Kimble family Come to Jesus. Even if he, too, had a bone to pick with Old Man Kimble. Griffin motioned to Logan that he was going to go.

But Mabel saw him and cut him off at the pass, her eyes pleading. *Stay*, she mouthed. If there was one thing Griffin couldn't do, it was say no to Mabel Ryerson.

Not again.

He lowered onto the chair at the sewing table, near where Logan sat on another wooden chair. A respectful distance, but he was there. To support Mabel or whatever she needed. Not because he wanted to, but because he had to. That was the thing about falling in love with someone. Even if it happened forever ago, that love never left. It stayed with you.

It stayed with Griffin. It was with him from the

moment he first met Mabel, when they were little kids playing in the front yard—him, Miles, and Logan trapping prairie dogs—and Mabel and Lucy would get in the way.

The other boys, they were downright angry with the girls, tattling and pretending they were going to trap the girls if they didn't bug out. Griffin, though, he was intrigued. Intrigued by Mabel's feistiness. By the fact that she hated the boys trapping 'dogs and actively protested it, a little animal advocate. Griffin never did stop trapping 'dogs that were eating the garden and crops, and he kept hunting. But those early interventions of Mabel's, well, they sure taught him to take it seriously. To treat animals, even pests, with a humanity that only a sweet young girl knew.

As the years went on and the kids all grew up, Griffin saw younger Mabel a different way. There was a phase where she bothered him. Not by virtue of anything she did, but it was her presence. When he was thirteen, waiting at the bus stop and a pretty schoolmate happened to be on the bus, Griffin didn't want Mabel hanging off his arm like a kid sister.

Then when she was fourteen and he was going on sixteen, there she was. Quieter than when she was younger. Bookish. Close to Lucy still, and her mother, too. Her grandmother. Shy, even. Closed off. But strong, too. And beautiful, in an enigmatic way.

Then she hit fifteen, and Griffin needed a date to the Winter Formal. Logan didn't seem bothered when

Griffin threw out Mabel's name. In fact, Logan had even said something along the lines, "Cool. Then we can all just go together. Easy."

And from that point on, it was easy. Easy and fun and exciting and everything in life that Griffin wanted out of a first love.

Maybe even out of a forever love.

It hadn't taken long for the teenage pair to exchange those heady words. It wasn't in the heat of passion, either. Griffin promised Logan and Logan's father he'd be every bit the gentleman that a father or son expected for the women in their lives.

What's more, Griffin promised his own father, too, that he wouldn't compromise the sacred relationship between their families. Griffin kept that promise, treating Mabel like a princess, which was easy.

She was, too. Mabel was his mischievous princess, bookish and shy and smart as a whip and unfazed by Griffin's rough-and-tumble hobbies like football and wrestling and throwing logs to help out at the base camp whenever his dad needed him.

They worked, Griffin and Mabel. There was nothing wrong.

Except that Griffin was graduating, and Mabel still had two years of high school ahead of her. For them to remain together was improper. At least, according to one, very concerned interloper who had wished to remain anonymous. Griffin would never forget the advice. *You've got your whole life ahead of you. Imagine if either of you were to meet someone who's better for you? Then what?*

It was a surprise and a hurt, to get such a lashing. He wondered if the person thought he wasn't good enough for Mabel? Or, worse, Mabel wasn't good enough for him? He hadn't been experienced enough to know what was what about the whole thing.

He remembered the sad feeling that came over him, then, but Griffin was only eighteen, and the secret advisor wasn't the only one putting the heat on Griffin to grow up and spread his wings. Seemed like every which way he turned, the signs were there. Even so, he ignored them.

Until Mabel forced his hand.

For everything that she was, quiet and unassuming and whip-smart and stubborn as a mule, the most critical trait of Mabel's was that she knew her mind. She wanted to marry Griffin. It was a warm, sunny day and they'd gone for a long drive. Mabel forced him to put an Elton John CD on, and she sang along to "I Guess that's Why They Call it the Blues" with all the passion of a woman who'd lived and loved and been burned, hard.

Little did either of them know, that's just what would happen. They'd burn each other. He, by telling her no, he couldn't just up and marry a sixteen-year-old. She by deciding that his refusal brought them to an impasse.

The memories swam in Griffin's head while the family settled into a heated discussion of what had brought Mabel back, why she was so upset, and why Logan was equally angry. Griffin wanted to tune it all out, but then if he was promising his old flame to have her back, he'd better follow along.

"Mabel," Logan went on. "Grandpa had Grandma Betty's diary all along. He'd been reading through them, and last night he called me."

Mabel looked plaintively back at her brother.

Old Man Kimble made a gargling noise, despite not having a drink that Griffin could see. All eyes turned on him, and he made his way through the garbling sound to say, "Mabel, I know you can't let go of your guilt."

It was a shock. A succinct, simple shock. How he'd said it. What he'd said.

Even Griffin felt his jaw hang open. He closed it and studied Mabel for her response.

She seemed stricken. The whole room, silent as a church, could hear her swallow and sniffle. Griffin could see the glistening of a fresh sheet of tears ready to spill over her cheeks. He wanted to spring from the sofa and cradle her. Griffin knew how she felt, not because he'd experienced it, but because it was the sort of thing he'd long to feel.

Ridiculous as it was, Griffin had only ever wished his family was close enough that a death like Betty's or Delilah's would tear any one of them apart. He didn't want Mabel to be torn apart. It was the last thing he wanted. But he understood. As best as he could, he understood.

Mabel, despite her brokenness, was still strong. "Grandpa, I'll *never* let go of my guilt." She was kneeling at his chair, and the old man leaned forward and braced a hand on her shoulder.

"She would want you to. Grandma Betty. And so would Delilah." His words and the thoughts behind them were so clear. Griffin saw this man through a new lens. He wondered just how appropriate it would be to ask Jim Kimble to help with the company. Would it be taking advantage? To play to his sympathies? Griffin wasn't sure now.

"It wasn't your fault, Mabel. But if you continue to carry that anger with you, then you'll never get over it. If I can move past Delilah's death—" Griffin watch Logan as he reached for Kelly's hand. A sweet gesture, but it probably stung Mabel. "—then you can."

"That's terrible logic. You weren't driving the car!" Mabel burst out. "You weren't the one! The reason!"

"You're taking responsibility for an icy roadway and the accidental death of an old woman," Jim pointed out softly.

"And a young woman," Mabel argued.

"She wasn't wearing her seatbelt," Logan sighed, low and painful.

Mabel's head snapped up. "You're blaming your wife!"

"She's gone, Mabel." Logan got up from his chair and joined Mabel on the floor and wrapped his arms around her. "She's *gone*. It wasn't Kelly's fault. It wasn't your fault or Grandma's or anyone's. It was an accident."

Mabel was crying, and Griffin wished he were the one holding her. He felt a compulsion to rip her from her brother and protect her, but he also knew that Mabel's heart would never recover from the accident. Not if she didn't face it like she was doing now. He knew deep down that this was what she needed.

It's what her family needed, too. It was just another thing Griffin observed that he wanted. And despite all of it—all the grief he was buried in, other people's grief—Griffin realized just how wrong he'd been to have ever told Mabel they couldn't marry. Maybe if he had, tragedy wouldn't have struck.

Maybe if he had, he wouldn't have lost her for good.

Chapter 18 — Betty

D ecember 20, 1984

Oh, Diary. Logan has become a pistol at the tender age of just two! He's not a troublemaker, but I won't be surprised if he ends up giving his mama and daddy trouble. That boy.

The sweetest thing, Diary. Today, Logan stayed with me while Nance went to her doctor's checkup. You remember she's pregnant again. A second little one. She and Norm are both swearing up and down that two will be IT for them. Can't say I blame them! Logan is a handful.

I'm working on an afghan for the baby. I've chosen yellow and gray for the colors, which happen to be the same colors I chose for Nancy when I found out I was pregnant with her. For Nancy's part, she's sewing an outfit for the little one to wear home from the hospital. By hand, mind you. She thinks if she sews it by hand, that it'll be a little more special. I told her that God didn't give us Singers for nothing, but Nancy was fixated on the task. Has been all week. So much so that she pricked her finger. It bled a little on the white fabric, and my! I have never heard Nancy utter a swear in her life, and there she was, blast-it-ing this and blessed-ing that and going so far as to take the Lord's name in vain.

I think the pregnancy is getting to her. Or maybe it's Logan. Did I mention he's a handful? Maybe for the second baby's delivery, I'll give the baby the afghan and I'll give Nancy a thimble. Ha-ha! And then there's Little Logan. He'll need a special treat, too, as the important big brother. I'm thinking for Logan I'll do a cross-stitch. It'll read: Frogs, snails And puppy-dogs' tails, that's what Logan is made of.

But do you know what, Diary? He already loves his little sister or brother. He says he wants a sister so he can take care of her. My hunch is that if they do wind up with a little baby girl, she'll be the apple of that boy's eye. He's got a soft and big heart. And do you know something, Diary? This little boy sure is quick to forgive. Just today, our poodle, Fifi, took one of his toys, and do you know what Little Logan said once I got the darn thing back? He said, "That's okay, Nama Betty," in his little boy speech. "That's okay. I not mad."

Well, I'll tell you something, if Logan is a forgiver,

then I brace myself to think of what the next baby will be. Doubly sweet? Or all spice? Hard to say.

Speaking of which, Jim and I are in a bad way, Diary.

If I still had my wedding ring, I'd have pulled it off in anger by now. But that ring graces Nance's finger. Maybe one day, it'll grace another woman's. Logan's wife? Or the new baby's, if she's a girl? In its place, I have a band that's too tight to yank off. So much for grand gestures of frustration!

I hesitate to even write this, because it's such a delicate, personal subject, a marriage. You know, just a few Sundays ago, the pastor spoke to the Ladies Auxiliary on the topic of marriage, in fact.

He told us that anything done in anger within a marriage is best soon lit afire. Somebody raised their hand, if you can even imagine, and questioned him. It was Gladys, of course! Gladys said, right there in the middle of the meeting in front of the entire group, she said, "I thought you were supposed to blow away your troubles like a dandelion. That's what my priest told us when we were married."

The pastor had an interesting reply. He said, "If you blew away your troubles, in a marriage or elsewhere, like a dandelion, then wouldn't they just grow and grow, like weeds, on your lawn?"

Gladys retorted, I'm sure you can believe. She said, "Well, even so, fire and brimstone have no place in a house of worship or within a marital bond."

He said, and I am getting this close to perfect because it stuck in my heart so solidly, "In this life, there is earth, wind, water, and fire. You can cast your problems to the earth for the future generation to dig up. You can blow them into the wind, to scatter and grow. You can drown them in water, for they will float back to the top. Or you can burn them to ash."

That's when Gladys said, and she was smug about it, "For you are dust, and to dust you shall return. Genesis."

Diary, I'm too simple a woman to understand it, but what I took from their back-and-forth was that problems never go away. Not really.

Anyway, I'm worried about us. Jim and me. Just worried, Diary. I think I'll go darn socks, because the Bible also happens to say something about idle hands.

Yours,
  Grandma Betty (almost twice over!)
  ***

  December 21, 1984

It's not often I get to steal away Diary time twice in one week. But here I am with an update. I feel a bit like a teenager to write this, but Jim and I are better. Turns out, all it takes to mend a marriage is something my mother would have called Grace. Well, grace and forgiveness.

I hadn't planned on getting into specifics, because our

argument was so bad. So dark. It was the sort, up until the morning, that I worried might change things.

I was wrong, though. And while it was a bad fight, it wasn't the last fight. I hope not, at least. And I bet that if I write it down, that I'll look back one day and see that this was one of many small things in a big life. That's my hope, anyway.

Here goes nothing.

I had to confess a secret to Jim. I'd been keeping it sealed over in my heart for too long, and with Nancy having her second baby, I couldn't stand it a moment longer.

I told Jim about how Nancy and Norm started dating in high school, against what we knew would have been his wishes. You see, he was angry as the devil, going so far as to call me a liar. I don't know that anyone in my life has called me a name, and it hurt. So I called him hard headed and old-fashioned. I called him a big, fat bore. Jim isn't fat, but his belly does stick out these days, and it was a low blow, as they say. Things got bad then worse, and he told me that if he'd known about Nancy and Norman back then, that he'd have forbade they get married.

You see, Jim had a high school sweetheart named Cloris. He feels very firmly, Diary, that had he married Cloris, he'd never have had a happy life. It took leaving high school and meeting me, his mother's friend's daughter, to find true happiness.

Diary, it was the most romantic excuse for anything I've ever heard of. Luckily, Norm and Nancy are two peas in a pod. They're the perfect match, happy as a set of clams and glowing over in love. If they weren't, I'd have such regrets. I'll tell you this, diary: it's something I'll never forget, Jim's earnestness over the whole matter. He probably has a point.

Well, that's all. Here I am, admiring my too-tight wedding band and dreaming of our new road back to happiness.

Thank God for small graces.
  Betty

Chapter 19 — Mabel

The crying was over. Mabel felt like it might even be over for good. Or, at least for a while.

Logan went to the kitchen and brought in two more chairs. "Mabel, Kelly, sit down." He looked at Mabel. "I'll explain everything."

Kelly winced. "Logan? Can I, actually?"

He looked at her surprised then at Mabel who was still unsold on their union and confused about why Kelly was even there now. Mabel simply nodded, more curious than angry, anyway.

Kelly shook her hair back, rolled her shoulders, and smoothed her hands down her thighs. "Mabel, I know we don't know each other. Not yet. I think, with time, you'll find out that we have a lot in common."

Mabel didn't agree.

"It's true. Did you know I'm taking up sewing?" Kelly asked.

"No. I don't sew anymore anyway."

"You don't?" Kelly frowned at her and glanced back at Logan, a silent accusation that he'd been wrong.

Mabel knew she didn't have to explain herself, but she did anyway. "I mean, I do. Not like I used to. Not for work. Just for fun now."

"Well, that's what I want to do it for. Fun." Kelly smiled. "Anyway, Mabel, your grandfather called Logan, and he said he found a request your grandmother had made in her diary. It wasn't long before she passed."

"What request? I read what Grandpa sent. There was no request made."

"Well, that one I felt like you should read in person," Logan interjected.

Mabel turned hot. "This was a trick? You sent me the diary entries to set me up? Lure me here?"

"No," Logan shot back. "Not at all. I mean—"

"Yes!" Grandpa declared, triumphant almost. "It *was* a lure. That's exactly what it was, Mabel." His voice was harsh and cold, like he was mad at Mabel.

She didn't want to cry again. She forced down a gulping swallow. "You wanted to lure me home?"

"Mabel," Grandpa spat her name out and leaned forward in his chair. He'd woken up some, come to life now. "Listen to me. I won't have you giving up on your family. We didn't give up on you. And the only way I knew how was to do that newfangled thing with the Facestory."

"Facebook, Grandpa."

"Face-what*ever*. Betty used it, and I remember she always talked about how you never wanted to be her friend. I didn't know she meant on the computer, but now I know. So I figured I'd show you just what's what. Your grandmother loved you to pieces, Mabel. She wanted you to have all of this. Every last bit of it!" He threw up his hands and breathed heavily, panting, before leaning back in his chair and falling quiet again.

Mabel looked back at Kelly. "You helped him, then?"

She nodded. "I know my way around Facebook. We figured out how to get into her account. I didn't want to be sneaky, but—"

"Why didn't you say anything when we were at the cottage? Like, right away? Why didn't you come out and say what you'd done?"

"Grandpa told us not to. He wanted to address it with you. We—well, Kelly—was the messenger, so to speak."

Mabel turned back to Kelly. "You were okay with interfering like this?"

"She wasn't interfering," Grandpa muttered. He heaved a long breath and leaned forward again. "Mabel, we know what you're doing. You're running away from us in order to run away from yourself."

"But we never ran away from you," Logan added.

Mabel's face went slack. Her heart pounded in her chest with a mixture of guilt and sadness and also, to a smaller degree, hope. "I know," she whispered.

"We love you," Logan said.

"I know," Mabel whispered again. Her eyes flicked to Griffin. "You weren't part of this?"

He shook his head. "No." She felt deflated. As if she'd tended to a smidgeon of hope that maybe Griffin was the cause of this. Maybe he wanted her back, and he was playing tricks and casting bait out to do that. But no, it was her oddball family with their oddball ideas.

She thought for a moment. "What was Grandma Betty's request? Where is it?"

Grandpa gestured to Logan, "It's over there." He pointed to his rolltop.

Logan opened the rolling door and sure enough, sitting squarely in the middle of the desk was a short stack of notebooks. A couple of them were ancient looking. Some were newer.

"It's the top one," Grandpa said.

Logan grabbed the one off the top, a little rectangular diary complete with a clasp. Over the cover were images of sewing accessories. Spools of thread. Needles with wide eyes. And, of course, thimbles. Grandma Betty loved her thimbles. A memory pooled into Mabel's brain. An early one. She must have been no older than five.

Mabel's mom, Nance, had dropped her off at Grandma's for the day. Logan was in school, but for whatever reason, Mabel was not. Maybe she hadn't started kindergarten yet. Grandma and Grandpa lived in their old house on Schoolhouse Lane, a little brick ranch style for which Mabel had strong, fond remembrances.

Grandma was giving Mabel her very first sewing

lesson. It was all things basic and simple, but Mabel could distinctly recall feeling very grown up. Very advanced under the watchful guide of her grandmother.

"We'll start with darning a sock," Grandma had instructed. For some reason—maybe it was the types of socks Grandma bought Grandpa—she was always darning socks.

"First, you'll want to set out your needle or stick it in the pin cushion, like this."

Mabel had grabbed at the needle, and sheering pain shocked her. She'd poked herself. A bead of ruby red blood had sprouted on the pad of her thumb. A wail had escaped her lips, and that wail had turned into a sob. "Gramma!"

"Oh, sweetie, here." Like a magician, Grandma had pulled a hankie out of thin air and masterfully dabbed the blood away. She then had wrapped the white hankie around Mabel's thumb and told her to wait. Grandma had left and was back in a jiffy with a brown bandage, which she fastened gently over the small wound.

"I'm never sewing again!" Mabel had cried.

"Hm." Grandma had taken Mabel's threat seriously, the little girl could tell. She'd tapped a finger against her chin thoughtfully. An idea had sprung to her head. "Mabel, I forgot something important. I'm terribly sorry." She'd looked terribly sorry. She pushed up from the chair at the sewing table and strode to a shelf where she'd kept supplies. Mabel had known about this shelf. She'd admired the little row of items along the top of it.

They'd reminded her of small bells. Grandma had plucked one of those bells and turned with it, then brought it to Mabel's bandaged thumb that, surprisingly, had stopped hurting. Just a weak throb at the tip, but Mabel had wondered if maybe the bandage was a little too tight. She was smart for five.

"Here we are," Grandma had said, and then she'd plunked that small silver bell onto Mabel's thumb. Mabel's look of confusion had been handily addressed. "That will protect your thumb when you're sewing. Ready to thread the needle?"

Mabel hadn't been ready yet, because she had a burning question: this thing on her thumb that sat like a loose helmet over her tiny finger. "What is it?" She'd given her grandma a thumbs up by way of showing the would-be bell.

"Oh, silly me. Mabel, this—" she tapped the side of the bell and Mabel's thumb "—is called a *thimble*." Then she pointed to the letters that little Mabel couldn't quite spell out. "And this here says *Kimble's Shoppe*. You see, sweetheart, this very thimble belonged to your grandpa's mom and dad when *they* owned our business. It's what you call a family heirloom. Family heirlooms are very important, Mabel," Grandma had remarked seriously.

And to her little self, Mabel thought, *Well, not quite as important as not pricking your thumb with a needle. It was a very good thing for thimbles.*

Chapter 20 — Mabel

Mabel accepted the diary from her brother and opened it, skimming just a handful of pages that had been filled. None were familiar. All were recent.

"It's this one." Kelly had come up behind her and pointed to the page that had been marked with a sticky note. The entry was dated November 2, 2019. There were three pages dedicated to this particular day.

Mabel looked up at Kelly then at Logan, at Grandpa. Finally, at Griffin.

Griffin asked, "Do you want some privacy?"

She shook her head. She really didn't. Mabel had spent the past two years fiercely clinging to privacy. She was ready for the opposite of that, whatever it was. Company, probably.

Mabel read the entry aloud.

"'Dear Mabel—'" her throat closed up. Mabel felt

like suffocating. This entry was for her. Just for her. But she read on, aloud. "'I've spent decades of my life maintaining my personal notes, but I hadn't once stopped to think about who might read them. How hollow of me. I'm sure Jim will, but Jim's been my husband. He's been privy to every secret I've ever held. I even confessed to him the ones I'd kept long, long ago. For example, did you know I told your Grandpa that I knew about your mother's first boyfriend? Oh yes, dear. Grandpa would have had a fit over Norm back then. Some things a woman, or a girl, keeps close to her heart until it's safe to let go of. There were other secrets, too. I told him that once, during a hard point in our marriage, I nurtured a flirtation with one of our dry cleaning clients. It never amounted to anything, this flirtation, but it was wrong of me. And it was wrong of the client, too. I spilled the beans to Grandpa, along with a list of other little missteps from my life. There was the time I forgot to pay the electric bill for three months straight. When the overdue notice came and our service was canceled that very afternoon, I blamed it on the postman. Do you know that your grandpa trusted me so much that he went down to the post office, demanded to speak with our mail carrier, and read him the riot act about overdue notices and bills? Grandpa always took my side, even when I was wrong. I made good on that poor postal man. I took him home-baked cookies and wrote an apology letter and made a private meeting with the postmaster to make sure the air was clear.

"Turned out the air didn't need clearing. Turned out I wasn't the first to blame late bill payments on the post office. Grandpa was none too happy when I later confessed my transgressions. But do you know what, Mabel? I paid for them, and I moved on. That's all you can do when you make a mistake in life.

"I suppose I'm writing all of this down as a bit of a final confession, because there is one more thing I want to get off my chest. It's something I need forgiveness for, but I'm too scared to ask for it in person, I suppose.

"I hope you'll forgive me, Mabel. Griffin went to your father and mother, Nance and Norm, and do you know what he asked them?" Mabel stopped reading. She pushed her mouth down in a frown and glanced up at Griffin. What had he asked her parents?

Griffin looked as bewildered and taken aback as anyone. He held up both hands and gave Mabel a shrug. "I—" Then, he looked at Logan. "Logan? What's this about?"

"Just keep reading, Mabel," Logan muttered.

Mabel looked back at the page, nervous about what she'd find there next. She cleared her throat. "Griffin asked your parents for your hand in marriage. Your mother confided in me, and I told her absolutely not. I told her that marriage is a difficult thing, and there is no sense in rushing. Mabel, you were only in high school. Way, *way* too young. You'd have wound up on the five o'clock news, a feature story that read *Teenage Bride of Brown County*. I wouldn't stand for it. I told your parents that if they consented to your young engagement, that I would never speak to them again.

"Mabel, I was an angry woman, then. I saw your life through my own glasses, which were fogged up with a lifetime of being a wife and allowing everything else to come after that. I put my marriage before everything to the ironic detriment of my marriage. I was worried that you'd do the same and if you did, and started so young, that you'd grow up and be bitter, even if it was a good man like Griffin was bound to become. And he did. Maybe I meddled when I shouldn't have. Actually, I know that I meddled when I shouldn't have. I made a mistake, and I'm sorry, Mabel. I hope you'll forgive me."

Mabel squeezed her eyes shut. Her world swirled around in her head—every decision she'd ever made. Every date she'd ever gone on. Every job she'd ever left because she figured she'd somehow not known herself well enough. It had all started with her high school heartache. Which was so crazy, but it *had*. Everything Mabel did could be traced back to how she saw herself after Griffin broke things off.

"Is that it?" Kelly asked this gently, her voice low.

Mabel opened her eyes, peering first at Kelly. She shook her head. Then, she let her gaze wander to Griffin. His jaw was clenched. His hands shoved in his pockets. Mabel didn't know if she should call him a wimp for accepting Grandma's wishes or a gentleman for respecting them.

She didn't know anything. Griffin looked helpless, too.

Mabel read on. "But I want you to know, Mabel, that even if you can't find it in your heart to forgive me, I'm going to be a little bit radical, as they say. I'm going to forgive myself. And I want you to know, if you grow into an old lady who meddles in her daughter's or grand-daughter's love life, and you come to regret it, or if you ever do anything you feel bad about, don't carry that hardness in your heart. Fix your mistake. Make your apologies. Clean your wound. Bandage it up. Then put a thimble on your heart and keep sewing, sweetheart."

Chapter 21 — Griffin

Griffin felt utterly helpless as Mabel dissolved into a puddle of tears. He watched with restraint as Kelly tried to comfort her only for Mabel to shake the well meaning woman off.

Logan, too neared her, but it was Mr. Kimble who swept Mabel into a tight embrace. The old man stood, seeming stronger now than he had before, and Mabel sobbed into his chest.

Griffin had no idea about Betty Kimble's influence. He had only ever figured it came from Mabel's parents, and he knew how close she was to them, back then. For Griffin, who understood what a close relationship with one's parents could mean, he had to weigh heavily his next step. He could tell Mabel that her mother and father forbade them to wed, and therefore turn their love story into some *Romeo and Juliet* elopement which wouldn't end well after all. Or he could do the gentle thing. The right thing.

Griffin could protect Mabel from the truth. He'd accept the weight of the responsibility. He'd tell Mabel that they were too young. Maybe they had been. He'd swallow his pride and Mabel's hurt and take it all.

And he did.

After a long few minutes, Mabel finally broke the embrace with her grandfather. "Did you know?" she asked him.

"That your grandmother tried to keep you from a bad decision?" Mr. Kimble's face went unreadable as he threw a look to Griffin. "Sorry, Son. But for a sixteen-year-old girl in the twentieth century, a teenage wedding *would* be a bad decision. You were too young then." He looked back at Mabel. "But, no. I didn't know. Betty kept some things close to her heart. Until she was ready to let them free. I think that's a trait you share with her." He smiled sadly.

Mabel, who was now somewhat consoled, turned to Griffin. "Did you know?"

His chest rose and fell. He scratched the back of his head and shoved his hand back into his pockets, then looked nervously at the others in the room. "Um, can we —" then he spoke directly to Mabel "—can I talk to you privately?"

Chapter 22 — Mabel

She wanted to speak with Griffin privately, too. But first, Mabel had to finish the business she'd really come to finish.

"On the way back to the cottage?" she replied to Griffin. "If you'll give me a ride, that is?" A small smile forced itself over her mouth. Almost magically, Mabel was feeling better. Good, even. She wasn't sure when she last felt as good as she felt right then.

"Of course." He nodded to Mabel then Logan and Kelly. But not before moving to Grandpa and offering a hand. "Mr. Kimble, I'd love the chance to talk to you, man to man, sometime soon."

Grandpa didn't seem too surprised. "Depends on the topic."

Mabel wondered if there wasn't more that Griffin would speak to Grandpa about. More than just the sale of his father's logging company.

Cryptically, Griffin replied, "Well, I sure could use some of those words of wisdom of yours."

Grandpa shook Griffin's hand and patted him on the shoulder. "How about coffee. Saturday morning?"

"Name the time and place. I'll be there," Griffin said.

"Seven sharp. Downstairs."

"Downstairs? You mean the coffee place on the corner?"

"No, I mean downstairs. You bring the coffee."

Griffin grinned. "I'll bring the coffee."

"Oh," Grandpa said, as Griffin turned to go. "One more thing."

"Sure?"

"Bring some super glue, too. For that lamp I broke."

Griffin laughed, and Logan and Kelly oohed and ahhed—gaining an answer to an unasked question they'd had about the broken glass downstairs. But Mabel's stomach twisted. Even just the reminder of the glass, of anything shattering, really affected her. She knew that talking things out with her family would never be enough to drown out the visceral reaction she had. There was only one thing, aside from continued medication and therapy, that would help.

Time.

Time and space. The good news was, Mabel had time. She had space.

Because her future had changed. Right then, in that moment, she knew that this wouldn't be her last visit to Prairie Creek or her last visit with Grandpa or Logan or even Griffin, probably. She'd come back. She'd be okay.

After Griffin had left, Kelly spoke first. "Maybe I'll go, too. You three need time to talk."

"Actually, I'd like if you stayed, Kelly." Mabel was earnest, too. If Logan was serious about her, or even if he wasn't—though she suspected he was—then Mabel had better accept Kelly as part of their world.

"Whatever you want," Kelly replied warmly. She was a comfort, just her presence. Mabel wouldn't have realized it had she not let her guard down, but she could see what Logan saw in this woman. An authenticity. A simple kindness. Maybe she was a little like Mabel, too.

"Kelly," Mabel began, realizing that the conversation had to start with where she felt the most recent bout of pain. "I'm sorry I ran away like that. I was close friends with Delilah. I take it you know all about Delilah?"

Kelly nodded, sadness filling her eyes. "Logan has told me everything. I know all of you loved her a great deal. She was your sister."

"Yes. She really was." Mabel looked at her hands. Without realizing it, she'd been knitting her fingers together, rubbing the pads of them as if she had a needle she was working through a thick swatch of denim. Muscle memory could do wonders on soothing one's nerves. "The car accident, well, it *was* an accident. But I blamed myself for it—obviously I still do." Mabel stole a glance at Grandpa. "I'm going to work on that, but it won't happen overnight."

"If I may," Kelly replied, "it sounds like everyone is giving you their permission. And I know Logan has said your parents most of all."

"They moved to Minneapolis," Mabel pointed out, not to be contradictory but to state a fact. They couldn't deal with what had happened either. They were angry and sad and heartbroken, too.

"Because they missed us, Mabel. I was in Minneapolis," Logan reasoned. "They couldn't stand to be here when both you and I had up and left."

Mabel swallowed. "Logan, how can you ever forgive me?"

"Because I love you," Logan answered instantly. "I forgive you, because I love you, Mabel. And because I know that God works in mysterious ways. That car accident was a tragedy, but as much as we loved Delilah, I know she loved us as much or more. She wouldn't want us to run away or put our lives on hold. She isn't coming back. Grandma isn't coming back. We can't change the past. We have to do what Grandma wrote in that diary."

"What?" Mabel asked, her chest tightening up again.

"We have to forgive each other, sure. But we also have to forgive ourselves."

Chapter 23 — Griffin

G riffin took the time alone to practice what he was going to tell Mabel, how he was going to explain to her that he was a coward back then. That he didn't love her enough to fight for her?

Well, he'd have to tell her the truth.

That he loved her enough to let her go, because if he hadn't, then they wouldn't have lasted.

Mabel, he muttered as he paced in front of the truck, *listen, what happened back then, I didn't have a choice.* He groaned and pushed his hands through his hair. Yes, he *did* have a choice, and he made his choice. He turned on a heel and started over. *Mabel, when I knew that we weren't going to have your parents' support, I had to give you up.* Ugh. Worse. Another groan.

He turned again, now tracking back in front of his truck a third time. *Mabel, back then, I was stupid. I never should have let you go. Regardless of your parents or anything anyone else said. I believed in us, but—*

"You made a good decision."

He whipped around.

Mabel stood in front of the shop. She smiled.

"Hey." He frowned. "Um, how'd it go up there?" He looked for Logan and Kelly.

"They're staying with Grandpa. Kelly is going to make him a light supper. It went well. I feel better than I have in a long time." She smiled.

"That's great." He went for the passenger door, "Here."

"Actually, can we walk and talk?" She indicated the sidewalk that trimmed Main Street.

They walked beside each other, close enough that their arms brushed with each stride. "Mabel, I don't know if this is the right time, but since we learned about your grandma's secret, I guess, if you want to call it that—"

"She wasn't wrong to do that. I mean, she *was*, I guess, but I get it. If I had a sixteen-year-old daughter who wanted to get married, I'd have said no. Any parent or grandparent would."

"I know. And it's my fault."

"How is it your fault?" She stopped and looked up at him. "I was the one who suggested it."

"You were braver than me."

"I was crazy."

"Are you still?" He pinned her with a stare. They

stood facing each other now, their bodies inches away. His heart raced in his chest. His pulse fluttered in that shallow spot beneath the skin of his neck. Griffin was aware of every square centimeter of the space he took up when he was with Mabel, even now, so many years later.

Mabel's expression was impassive. He couldn't tell what she was thinking and whether it was about him or her grandfather or the messages.

"Probably," she whispered, and then, his eyes fell to her hand which disappeared into her bag. When she withdrew it, she held her phone. Her gaze fixed on the screen and she tapped a few icons, then she held the phone to her ear.

Griffin could hear the ring of the line, that false sounding trill meant to emulate a real phone but cut a shrill chime that nagged the air.

Faintly, he heard Lucas answer Mabel's call.

"Where are you now? Are you still there?"

She fixed her stare on Griffin while she spoke to her fiancé. "Yes."

"When are you coming back?"

"You're not on your way?" she asked him. It might have been a dig, but on Mabel's sweet tongue, it sounded more like heartache.

Griffin couldn't make out Lucas's response, but the hitch in Mabel's voice and the stitch of her brows told him that whatever it had been had let her down. He was a fool, Lucas.

"I need to spend more time with my family."

Now, Griffin could hear the guy's answer. He'd raised his voice to nearly a yell. "If you think I support that, you're wrong."

"You could come here, Lucas. And get to know them. You could help me work through this."

"They're toxic people, Mabel!"

"Why?" She broke eye contact with Griffin, bit her lip and twisted forward, and Griffin walked alongside her again. "Why would they be toxic?" Then, she hit speaker. "You're on speaker, Lucas."

"Is someone else there?"

"Griffin is."

A silence. Mabel was brave, but Griffin wondered if there wasn't another underlying emotion pulsing through her heart. A will to be honest? Not only with Lucas or Griffin but with herself, too?

"Why are you doing this?" his voice was gentler now, but Griffin knew when someone was playing along, and Lucas was playing along. Saving face. If there was face left to be saved.

"I'm going to spend more time here."

"How? You've got work."

"I'm coming home tomorrow. I'll pack my bags and ask for a leave of absence. Then I'm going to come back. Do you want to come with me?"

Griffin frowned at her. Was she really inviting him?

"Of course not," Lucas spat. "Take me off speaker."

This was his chance, Griffin realized. This was a chance Mabel was granting her fiancé to prove out his love. Did she really love him? Griffin was desperate to ask Mabel this.

But he didn't get the chance.

Mabel took Lucas off speaker and pressed the phone to her ear. She nodded. Her eyes stayed straight ahead. They passed the post office. The pet groomer. The next storefront was Maisie's Bakery. Griffin eyed the place and made a last-minute plan to invite Mabel to join him for a lemonade or an iced tea, maybe a croissant. She made noncommittal sounds into the phone. *Mmhm. Uh-huh. Yeah.*

Mabel came to a stop just before the door to the bakery. Griffin started mentally rehearsing his apology again. She ended her phone call, muttering a goodbye into the line. She looked up at Griffin, but instead of a triumphant smile or a nervous giggle or any sign that they were about to *maybe* reunite, Mabel chewed her lower lip. Her eyes were a strange mix of sad and confused and sorry and also...hopeful?

"What did he say?" Griffin asked her.

Mabel took a beat before responding. He was about to invite her into Maisie's, but finally, she answered him. "Lucas is going to come."

Panic streaked up Griffin's spine. "What? He's going to come where?"

"Here. To Prairie Creek."

Chapter 24—Mabel

A sick feeling welled in her stomach as Griffin drove Mabel back to the cottage in silence. Everything was better now. She and Logan made up. She was ready to accept Kelly into the fold. And things with Griffin felt...healed.

But now this.

Griffin's truck was filled with a silence so suffocating that Mabel cracked the window and leaned her head against it, feeling the wind twirl her bangs.

Once they got to Melba's, Griffin jumped out and opened her door. "Are you going to leave now?"

"No." She'd stay the night. It was getting late. The sun had dipped below the horizon, now, and Mabel didn't like to drive under any conditions that could turn dangerous.

"Do you have a key to get in?" Griffin indicated the cottage.

"No. I'll wait until Logan gets back. And Kelly." The idea they were a pair rocked Mabel's world, still.

"I'll wait, too. I'm not going to leave you alone."

"It's fine. You can go, Griff." She closed the door behind her and held her bag against her front. "Grif*fin*."

He sighed. "Mabel, I'm not leaving you here alone. Anyway, you never let me—it's just...there was something I wanted to tell you before." He shoved his hands in his pockets and looked at her like he was mad or something.

Mabel started for the front porch. "Okay. Well, you can still tell me. Nothing's changed between us, Griffin." She gave a short, nervous laugh.

"Everything's changed, Mabel." But he said it in a soft, kind way, as though he was sad. Maybe she was, too.

They waited on the front porch, Mabel with her legs crisscrossed in the hanging wooden swing and Griffin leaning grumpily against a wooden column, for what felt like hours. The sun sank down below the far side of the earth. Crickets started in on the chirping melodies. Lightning bugs lit up a patch of the prairie grass just beyond the porch. Mabel loved lightning bugs. She hated that she couldn't enjoy them.

Finally, maybe an hour after a quiet wait, headlights flashed to life down the main road, growing brighter as Logan's truck grumbled through the moonlit prairie sky.

Everything right then felt like home, way more than Fargo ever could. Here, in Prairie Creek, even under the cover of night, there was a comfort to the place. The sort of comfort Mabel had longed for these past two years. Maybe even longer, because even before the accident, Mabel hadn't felt settled. She hadn't felt happy, maybe. Even with a good friend like Delilah and a stable existence of doing odd sewing jobs here or working nightshifts there. Even once she met Lucas...something was wrong.

Griffin shifted. "Here he comes."

Logan's headlights illuminated a moving cloud of dust as it rolled down the drive.

Mabel got up from the swing. Her body felt tired. "Thanks for staying and waiting, Griff," she said.

He looked at her. "I guess you'll be back soon, then?"

"Yeah. This weekend, probably."

"Right. Well, I'd better go then. I have a meeting this weekend, and I'd better get ready for it."

Mabel smiled. "Oh, of course. With Grandpa." She wanted to ask him if she'd see him when she was back, but Mabel knew the answer deep down. If it were her, and Griffin had a fiancée and they came back to town, Mabel would hide. Griffin skipped down the steps. "Griff, wait."

He looked back up at her, anticipation hanging in the cool air between them. Mabel moved to the steps and wrapped an arm around the column Griffin had just left. His presence was heavy around her. "Can I give you a tip?"

"A tip?"

"For when you meet with Grandpa, I mean."

He braced his hands on his hips. "Sure."

"He never really cared much about the logging thing. He only supported it because he was friends with your grandfather."

"You don't think he'll want to save it?"

"Grandpa cares about Prairie Creek. Just like Susan Gentry. But there could be another way."

"What do you mean?"

"Your goal is to keep an industry alive, right?"

"Keep my legacy alive."

"What if instead of saving the logging company, you bring a different one back to life?"

"What company?" He pretended to be impatient, but his body language said otherwise. He squared his shoulders to her and pushed one hand into the back pocket of his Wranglers.

"Kimble's Sew 'n' Vac."

Chapter 25 — Griffin

Griffin had slept on Mabel's idea that first night. It was wild. He had no experience with, or interest in, vacuums, sewing, or laundry. When he woke up the next morning, he pushed it away. He couldn't fix vacuums or sewing machines. He didn't want to deal with washers and dryers.

Mostly, though, he wanted nothing to do with the heartache that now irreversibly attached itself to the Kimble family as a whole. Even visiting Mr. Kimble was going to be painful, in the wake of knowing that Mabel had run back into the arms of Lucas.

Mabel's idea wouldn't work. Griffin had to save Dempsey & Sons, and that was that.

Anyway, what about Susan Gentry and Dolores and all that Griffin had helped his father build? What about all the years and work he'd put into logging? If he left that, then what were the last two decades for? They'd have been all in vain.

Before heading to Mr. Kimble's the next morning, Griffin swallowed down a plate of toast and eggs, gave Sam a bath, then called someone he hadn't expected to talk to for a long while.

He called his dad.

"Aloha!" Fletcher Dempsey cried over the phone.

"You're in Hawaii now?" Griffin asked. Sam snored in his favorite spot at the back door. Griffin let him rest. The poor thing was whooped.

"No! The Bahamas!" His old man lifted his voice over loud background noise.

"It sounds like you're at a nightclub, Dad. And it's —" Griffin checked his watch "—ten after six in the morning. Which has to be close to your time zone anyway."

"Tropicaerobics class!" Fletcher shouted.

Griffin smirked. "You guys have hit the ground running. You just got there!"

"Days ago!" Fletcher yelled. "But yeah! Griff, this place is the bee's knees. Really, we are *so* happy! How's P.C.?"

"P.C.?"

"Prairie Creek, my man!"

Who was this person? Certainly not the dusty, old-school lumberjack Griffin had grown up with. "Oh. Right. Can I talk to you, Dad?"

"Now? I'm in class!" Griffin overheard his dad

shouting at someone there, probably Tammy. "*I'll be right back. It's Griff! I know, Babe! One-two count. One-two count! I'll be back!*" After several seconds, Fletcher returned to the line, huffing and puffing and so out of breath, Griffin wondered if he might just keel over. Images of his dad being hauled in a crude wooden casket to an island airport, soaring over tropical skies and across the quilted land of middle America below—

"Okay. Whew! I'm here. What's going on, Griff?"

"It's the company. The sale and my attempt to, I don't know, save it, Dad. Save the business."

Fletcher blew out a long sigh. "Yeah. I talked to the guys."

"Who? Bill?"

"And Steve. Word gets around. Dolores is probably to blame. She couldn't hold on to a piece of gossip if it was super glued to her hand. Anyway, I don't blame you for wanting to keep it, Son."

"Do you want me to keep it?" This was the first moment it had occurred to Griffin to ask his father such a question. Maybe all along his old man was waiting for him to show a more powerful interest.

"Why would I have sold it if I wanted you to keep it, Griffin?"

"Because that's what Tammy wanted you to do." Griffin knew this to be truth as much as he knew foxes chased pheasants.

"Well, she's not disappointed, that's true. But if you think I sold our business for the whims of Tammy, you'd be wrong. You know what she thought I ought to do?"

"What?" Griffin hardly cared.

"Tammy said to give the whole shebang to you, Griff."

Anger rushed to Griffin's head. Now he was really bound and determined to convince Mr. Kimble to help him keep the thing. "If that's true, then why didn't you? Or why didn't you tell me that's what she said!"

"Griffin, not once did you show even a blush of curiosity in the company. You worked hard for me, I'm not saying you didn't. That's why you get the lion's share of proceeds, if you read the paperwork."

Small comforts.

His dad continued, "Do you remember when you first started on for me? What you said then?"

Griffin scoffed. "I was twenty. Maybe nineteen. I have no idea what I said, Dad."

"You said you never wanted to be a logger. You hated working the woods." His dad laughed. "You weren't soft. Still aren't. But you were a tinkerer, Griff. Don't you remember? That club you joined in high school, what was it? Robot club?"

"Young engineers."

"Right. You tinkered."

"But I never went to college. Didn't want to. I like blue collar work. You know that. I like Prairie Creek. I've seen the world. Done my traveling and exploring. I know what I want, and it's here."

"What is *it*, though? Cleaning the machines and fixing them. But you don't have to own a logging company to fix stuff, least of all heavy machinery. Or any machinery." Fletcher sighed again. Griffin wondered where he was on his new tropical island and what he might be looking at. The ocean? "Griff," his dad went on, and Griffin could tell this was the conclusion to their phone call, "I want you to do whatever makes you happy with whoever makes you happy. I wish someone had told me that when I was your age. Instead of following in my dad's footsteps or marrying the girl I'd met in high school. That's what was expected of me then. It was the next logical thing. But happiness isn't always logical, Son."

"So you're saying I should move to Japan or something?"

"What? Griff, *no*. I'm saying, do what makes you happy. Not what you think others think will make you happy."

Griffin had another question. "Does Tammy make you happy, Dad?"

"Tammy is my soulmate. I loved your mother, Griff. Heck, I still do! But Tammy and I—we were meant to find each other."

"Because she's pretty?" Griffin scoffed, but the chip on his shoulder was starting to dissolve.

"There is no reason I can give you that'll make sense. I love Tammy, and I love being with her. That's all there is to it."

"Did you love logging, Dad?"

"Heck, Son. It paid the bills. It made my dad proud. It gave you money in the bank. I'm grateful for logging. But do you know what I always want to do?"

"What?"

"Travel, kiddo. I wanted to see the world and feel the ocean on my sandy feet."

"You could have done that as a logger, Dad."

"Griffin, when you own a business in the woods, it's hard to see the forest for the trees."

Griffin considered this for a moment. "I just want to be in Prairie Creek. It's home. And I'm not sure what else I can do there to make any money." He felt pathetic. Even a little bit victimized, despite the fact that Griffin knew that was ridiculous. But he couldn't help the way he felt. Abandoned. Lost. Sad as heck. "And anyway, what about all those years I spent on logging?"

"For a man who wants to take over his father's business, you don't know that much about business, Son."

"What?" Griffin set out a bowl of kibble for Sam, who tore himself away from his nap long enough to gobble it down.

"First of all, that's called the sunk-cost fallacy. Just because you spent time on something, you think that means you have to stick to it. It's silly is what it is. But second of all, the years weren't wasted. When we sell the company, we stand to make a pretty penny. That money can tide you over, Griff. Help you find your next love or start your next business."

Images of Mabel and Mr. Kimble and the yellowing shop on Main Street pushed their way up through his head. It'd be too hard. Too heartbreaking.

But did his dad have a point? Was there wisdom beneath the tanned, glistening-with-sweat exterior of a retiree doing grapevines to the oldies down in the tropics?

There was only one way to find out.

Chapter 26 — Mabel

Saturday morning, Mabel was back, just as she'd said she'd be. A few weeks later than planned, but still.

Leaving her car in the drive, she followed him up to the porch.

Kelly waited there.

"Oh, Mabel," she beamed. "I'm so happy you're going to stay with us. Come in! Come in!"

The two followed Kelly into the cottage.

Seeing it again now, in the light of day and in the light of her own personal peace and happiness, Mabel was overwhelmed. The cottage felt every bit the same as when Aunt Melba was alive, but there was the feel of a facelift. Of a freshness. Of *life*.

"We're working on painting and refinishing the stairs," Kelly explained. "Oh, come see your room. You're going to *love* it."

They moved down the hall to the first bedroom on the right. Mabel recalled there had always seemed to be a lot of rooms in Aunt Melba's house. She'd never even counted them, because it was as if each time she visited, she learned that another nook, cranny, or full-blown bedroom appeared.

She stepped through a white-painted wood door with a crystal knob and was transported through time and space. The iron-framed bed, double in size, wore a white quilt, which hung neatly beneath a lace-trimmed duvet. Cool, tan linen sheets were tucked tight. Matching blue bedside tables offered a splash of color, but on each sat a crystal-trimmed lamp.

Beneath the picture window, a porcelain pitcher was centered inside of a shallow basin. A little wash table, like something out of an Amish homestead.

The wardrobe, heavy wood, anchored the room opposite the bed. Mabel opened the doors. Inside hung a spare quilt. On the shelf, neatly folded flannel ones. Winter sheets. A heavy duvet rested beneath an extra pillow.

Mabel turned from the wardrobe and spotted a familiar dresser along the wall. White with brass knobs and six wide drawers. She gasped. "That was *mine*."

"Melba had it moved here once your parents moved away. Logan told me it was yours. He has a good memory."

Tears filled Mabel's eyes. She looked at Kelly. "Thank you. This is—" she was speechless and waved a hand at the bedroom. Finally, she managed a small, "*perfect.*"

"Let me show you around, come on."

The trio left the bedroom and toured the others, all equally charming and perfectly appointed. All featuring touches of Melba and familiar furniture but revived with fresh paint and hardware and accessories that the modern traveler would appreciate.

In the kitchen, which hadn't yet changed—and Mabel thought really shouldn't—Kelly had set up lunch. "BLTs on rye," she said as she uncovered a plate of picture-perfect sandwiches complete with little sandwich swords poking out. "And," she lifted a second dish, uncovering it with a flourish, "fruit salad. We've got lemonade or ice water to drink, and we'll take the meal in the dining room. Will you help me, Mabel?"

Mabel looked at her chaperone who nodded them on into the dining room. Little had changed in there, save for the curtains. "Are these new?" Mabel asked Kelly, fondling the sheer white fabric.

"Just washed and mended is all!" Kelly answered brightly.

"Mended?" Mabel gave her a suspicious look.

"I did my best. Still learning! But that's why I have *you* here now." Kelly winked at her. "Speaking of which, are we still going to town after lunch?"

Mabel nodded. She'd made arrangements to visit Grandpa for an afternoon of coffee and cookies. Once there, she'd be collecting all of the things that Grandma Betty had left Mabel.

The three of them ate and chatted. Mabel learned more about Kelly, who had no children and had never been married.

"Almost once," she said once they were finishing up.

Mabel smiled, knowingly.

"You think you'll stay in Prairie Creek for good?" Mabel asked her, pushing the boundaries of their familiarity.

But Kelly was comfortable and confident and assured when she said, "Absolutely. I'm happy here." A big smile spread over her mouth as she looked at him and took his hand.

Logan squeezed it. "You'd better stay. I need you."

They'd become, in a short matter of time—well, a couple of months—closer than Mabel ever could have imagined. A handsome couple with similar goals, Kelly and Logan were as happy as Mabel would want her brother to be.

"Before we go," Kelly said, referring again to their trip into town, "we want to show you the barn and the pens.

"That's right. Logan said you have two goats." Mabel was curious about this. Livestock seemed to be a big commitment.

"I'm going to make soap from their milk. We're looking at dairy cows, too. That's our next big purchase."

Our. *Our.* Wow. Was it envy that stirred deep inside of Mabel?

Kelly must have seen it flash over her face, because she said, "You know what? We can do a tour of the farm when we come back. Let's get you to Grandpa Kimble's."

Chapter 27 — Griffin

Three weeks into the New Plan, as Griffin was calling it, and things were going more smoothly than he could have imagined. It turned out that working for a logging company prepared a man for quite a lot. Even smaller shops, such as this.

Plus, he got to bring Sam along to this worksite. It wasn't as dangerous for a dog as a logging operation.

The sale of Dempsey and Son had been finalized—with Susan Gentry's and even Dolores' blessings. It helped that Dolores was hired by the outfit from Fargo who had acquired it. And, since the jobs often took the business to various forests around the region, the new owners didn't need to keep an office in Prairie Creek. Dolores would work remotely. Though Griffin was disappointed that the town would lose a great employer and industry, he had high hopes that there were other opportunities to come.

He, himself, was creating just that.

Presently, he was spending that Saturday on the backroom. This was his co-investor's idea, even though Griffin figured they should get the exterior and front desk completed first. But having a mentor, as Griffin now did, he was obligated to trust the process. And the process meant whiling away the morning with a Thermos of coffee in a small space at the back of the shop. Mostly, the job required cleaning and oiling. Renovations and upgrades would come later, and in some cases not at all. In fact, the old man preferred that Griffin focus more on restorations than renovations.

That's where Kelly Watts had come in. Griffin came to appreciate her eye for detail and style. Plus, with his knowledge about running a business—information gathered from regular phone calls with his dad for advice—things were moving in the right direction.

In fact, it was looking as though they could open their doors to the public—or *re-open*, technically—as soon as the first autumnal leaf had dropped.

After grabbing a quick bite at Maisie's, he strode back to the shop, using his recently earned master key to let himself in through the front, where Sam had been napping, as usual. Griffin could go in through the back. There was a small mudroom there, and he could quickly hang his coat—when the weather turned—and stow his truck keys in his locker. But Griffin liked going in through the front better. Now that he was co-owner of a brick-and-mortar storefront, as opposed to a doublewide office and roaming lumber operations, he felt it important to take in the front every single time he entered the place.

He'd only just recently bladed off the remnants of decades old lettering that predated his entrance into the business. He'd done away with the *Open* sign, which was a later add but didn't quite hit the notes they were going for. In its place, he'd use an older version that had been stowed in the storage room that ran adjacent to the mudroom. It was black and white, although the white was crackling over in rust, and it read *Open for Business*, which reminded Griffin of a children's song he'd sung for a school play way back when he was in just the first grade and the idea of ever so much as working for a business had yet to cross his rascally mind.

But the new-old sign would have to wait a little while longer. For now, the back of it faced forward. *Sorry we're Closed!*

He closed and locked the door behind himself and made his way through to the back. His business partner was due down soon, for their usual afternoon coffee and check-in. It was upon Griffin to explain how everything was going, every day. What he'd accomplished. Who he'd hired out for what. Where they were in the timeline, and what they needed to acquire, still.

The lists were dwindling every day, but today Griffin had more questions than usual. The backroom and all of its accoutrements weren't exactly his forte.

He slipped in there and sat at the machine he'd most

recently begun work on. It was a National brand, and the basics of repair on this machine were similar enough to the other two that had been left in the shop. Currently, he was trying to replace the small lightbulb. No easy task when he wasn't sure a Singer model bulb would fit a National machine.

Griffin heard a rattle from beyond the little back room. "Mr. Kimble?" he called out, setting the bulb on the edge of the sewing table.

But absent was the older man's wheezing. Instead, the rattle persisted for another moment until the distinct chime of the bell that hung above the door could be heard, plain as day, even back where Griffin said.

"Hello?" he called out, wiping errant oil from his hands with a rag and standing. So far as Griffin knew, there was only one other person who had a spare key to the place. Logan.

"Logan? Is that you, buddy?"

A call came back. "Yep!"

Griffin relaxed and moved back to his seat. "I'm back here working on the machines!" He went on, half to himself half to his friend, talking and rambling as he tinkered. "Your grandpa wants this room done first, but I'm not exactly sure why. Seems to me we'll still have to hire a tailor before we can open up this part of things, and that'll be last, since I don't know a single person— other than Kelly, of course—who can sew a patch on an elbow. Anyway, what are you—" When Griffin looked up, his words fell away. His jaw hung open. His eyes crinkled in confusion. "What are you doing here?"

Chapter 28 — Mabel

M abel felt as confused as Griffin looked. "What are *you* doing here?" She turned to her brother and Kelly, but they shrugged.

Logan said. "We'll be upstairs with Grandpa. You two take your time."

It was a trap. A sweet one, but a trap still. She turned back to Griffin then let her eyes sweep over the room. Enchantingly, familiar sheer, yellow curtains rippled against a small window that gave a view to the meadow that ran behind Main Street. One wall was not a wall, but a unit of sturdy wooden shelves. Stacked there were tins with black letter labeling. Thread—blues. Thread—reds. Thread—black. Thread—white/cream/ivory. And more of the same. Some of the tins stowed other things. Tools. Fabric shears. Rotary cutters. Seam rippers. Measuring tapes. Pins and cushions. Every last item dredged up faint memories of Mabel's own grandmother, sitting in this room, even as an elderly, fragile woman, working away. Mabel could see her now, seated at a new, white Singer. She had preferred new to antique, citing the distinct absence of anyone who *really* knew how to fix machines (apparently Grandpa Kimble wasn't so adept). She'd be there, the glow of the sewing machine light soft on her crinkled face. Bifocals hung low on her nose. Her hair was pinned back, white curls like marshmallow pillows carefully secured away from the project at hand.

"Griffin?" Mabel whispered this and took a step into the backroom of her grandparent's old shop.

He seemed frozen in time and place. But slowly, a smile crept over his mouth. "Mabel. You came back."

She forced herself to move again, another tentative step in. Naturally, Mabel hoped—even *expected*—to run into Griffin. She'd had fantasies of contacting him and asking him out for coffee, as friends, maybe. Secretly, deep down, the truth was that Mabel had returned to Prairie Creek not only for family but also for Griffin Dempsey. "I said I would come back," she replied at last.

It looked like he was about to reach out to her, with both arms. At the last moment, though, he slipped his hands into his front pockets. He'd been sitting at a heavy-looking black sewing machine. She pointed to it. "What are you doing?"

"Trying to bring this old girl back to life."

"Why?"

"That way we don't have to buy all new machines. Our goal is to have three of them in good working order.

One day, we'll streamline with updates, same brand, same units. For now, we want to keep costs low until we know if we can make money with this end of the business—" he stopped short. "I'm rambling. Sorry."

She squinted and pushed her bangs off her forehead before spinning in a careful circle. The room was not only how she remembered it but also cleaner. Fresher. Like it could open up for business tomorrow, if it wanted to. "What?" she asked him again. "I don't understand." She was facing Griffin again and had moved her hands to smooth an apricot romper she'd made just the week before. Her final project in Fargo, before she'd packed everything to come home.

For good.

Before Griffin, Mabel felt small but strong. She took another step forward.

He did the same. "You didn't know?"

"Know what?" she asked. They were just a foot away from one another.

"About..." he turned and waved toward the room, indicating its rebirth and his place inside of it. "This. Me?"

"You?" She edged forward half an inch but twisted left as if to look for something that was missing. Something *was* missing from the shop room, but Mabel knew what it was and that she wouldn't find it there. Not yet, at least.

He rubbed the back of his head, and his dark hair fell forward over his face. He shook it back and pulled his other hand from his pocket. "Can I—can I--?" he held his arms out and stepped closer again.

Mabel matched his movement, entering into Griffin's embrace and pressing the side of her face against his chest. She inhaled deeply. He smelled like rust and wood shavings. Griffin held her tight for just a second before releasing her again. "It's great to see you again. I—I missed you." He said this with a wave of guilt, but Mabel knew that Griffin didn't know. Would he ask?

"How long are you staying for?"

"Um," she pursed her lips playfully. "Forever, basically."

He frowned. "Huh?"

Mabel reached again for Griffin, grabbing his hands. She'd wanted to do that since the last time she was there. Since she left them. Probably since long before that, in fact. "I'm back for good. I'm moving into the cottage with Logan. I'll help them for a while before I find my own place. I just—after the last visit, with things sort of settling and—"

Behind him, a miniature crash exploded, cutting through the air. Mabel flinched briefly then looked with curiosity around Griffin's legs at the source of the small shatter. "Oh no. Let me guess, a sewing bulb?"

He followed her gaze to spy the tiny white shards splayed across the tile flooring. But instead of taking up a nearby dust broom and pan, Griffin studied Mabel more closely. "You're okay?"

"Okay?"

"With that sound. Just weeks ago, you were covering your ears and shrinking away. You're not...scared now?"

She smiled. "I mean, it's not a pleasant sound, no. But it wasn't too loud. And I'm better. I really am. I'm *getting* better, I mean." And she was. Her therapist had recommended a moderate course of explore therapy, coupled with their twice-weekly regular routine and her medication. However, Mabel had come to suspect that it wasn't listening to YouTube videos of glass breaking that had made the difference in her recovery.

"You are." He wasn't asking. He was telling her. "I'm happy for you, Mabel." Griffin hesitated and glanced past her. "How does Lucas feel about living in Prairie Creek?" He was making mighty assumptions.

"He's not," she answered, playing around the heart of the matter, if for a moment.

Griffin closed their gap again and lowered his face. "He's not living here *now*?"

"Or ever," she replied, running her tongue over her lips. There it was again. The smell she'd come to miss after so short a while.

"What do you mean?" he frowned, but his hands had found hers again and they were dancing together at their sides. Mabel's chest heaved in shallow swells.

"I mean we broke up. Right after I went back to Fargo. Weeks ago."

"You never told me?"

She grinned. "Sometimes, you've got to keep things from people to protect them."

"Oh?" He was smiling too, and his fingers had interlaced with hers. Their palms pressed together. "Where'd you get that idea?"

"From a person who knew the value of patience."

"A few weeks doesn't exactly compare to two decades," he pointed out.

"I never could have waited two decades." Her face had fallen more serious now, and she chewed her lower lip all while staring breathlessly at Griffin's.

He dropped his mouth to her ear and whispered, "You already did."

Mabel was tired of contradicting people. She was tired of being on the outs or at odds or against. She was tired, most of all, of being unhappy. So instead of teasing him back, she turned her face to his and while his mouth was still hovering so dangerously close to hers she pressed into it, kissing Griffin deliciously. The taste of him was as much a memory as it was a present thing. Years and years disappeared like a slip stitch. There was no then and now, no other loves or engagements. There were no rejections or delays. There was only Griffin and Mabel. And as their lips moved in sync with their hands—hers sliding around his neck as she drew herself closer to him and his curling around her waist as he drew her to him—Mabel knew that if her family could forgive her, then she could surely forgive Griffin. And most importantly, she could forgive herself.

Chapter 29 — Griffin

Summer had flown by like a newly wound bobbin. Griffin didn't even mind that he thought about his world in terms like that—there were any other number of expressions he might use. As fast as the brush rollers on an Oreck, flying across hardwood. As fast as a washing machine at the end of its spin cycle. He loved all of it.

Mostly, though, he loved Mabel and their rekindled romance. It was more than that, of course. More than a romance. More than a high school sweetheart thing or a one-that-got-away thing. Their love was *everything*. And everything was sewn up in their love. Even their work.

The grand opening of the temporarily named "Kimble and Dempsey's Sew 'n' Vac" was slated for October 1. With Kelly's and Lucy's help, Mabel had the whole thing planned as precisely as the prick of a fresh needle. They'd ensured the event would coincide with the final Saturday sidewalk sale, so that they'd lure the most traffic. Typically, the sidewalk sales meant that every single merchant on Main Street had their wares out, and for the *final* one, it was even more of a push to liquidate ahead of winter and pheasant hunting season and all the changes that befell South Dakota in late autumn.

Beyond the comings and goings of Saturday-sale traffic, Mabel had planned to offer a few membership plans for dry cleaning and laundry services, which included delivery. Her plan was to double down on the foundation her grandpa and grandma had lain so long ago. In addition to the basic package, Mabel would offer pressing, steaming, and folding in addition to tailoring and mending. She'd run the sewing shop out of the backroom, and once they'd gotten their footing, they'd hire help.

Meanwhile, Griffin's job was all mechanical. Over the ensuing months, he'd started to learn about all the kinds of repairs the shop would require. It wasn't so hard, and he liked to tinker, especially when there were no computer boards involved. And with the equipment they used right now, there was none of that. Parts could be cleaned and fixed and replacements were minimal. It was the way Griffin remembered things used to be, and he liked that. In all aspects of his life, apparently. And Sam enjoyed napping near the comforting whirs of the smaller machines.

For the grand opening, Griffin was supposed to be helpful, which he figured he could manage. He could answer simple questions and hang around looking like a useful local as well as the face of a family who knew about business.

In fact, Griffin's own three parents had arrived for the occasion, his mom, Sheena, decked to the nines as always, and his dad and even Tammy. They'd burned themselves out early on their attempt to make a life in the Bahamas.

"Mostly, they don't really hunt down there, and I couldn't see myself coming out the hot side of winter without a freezer full of bird meat," Fletcher bragged to Griffin, Logan, and Miles, whose attention he held captive while Mabel scurried around, courting visitors and potential customers alike.

Griffin kept his eye on Mabel, who moved like a bird, flitting from a clique of guests to a clique of friends or family. She was in her element, and it was nothing short of inspiring to see her in this new role as a leader and an artist—she wore a beautiful, cashmere cranberry-colored blouse (she'd taught him all about things like the nuance of fabric colors and types) and tweed slacks. Griffin, meanwhile, was dressed in the Prairie Creek menswear uniform: a flannel button-down and Wranglers. He might be seriously committed to a seamstress and garment maker, and he might own a business that dealt heavily in clothing, but simple was his way.

Tammy sauntered over from her strained-but-polite chit-chat session with Griffin's mother. "Hello, boys," she drawled. Griffin expected her to be disappointed about not living out her final years in TropicAerobics classes and sand-exfoliation spa treatments. Instead, though, she flaunted her exotic adventure mercilessly, wearing unique, revealing island garb even now, when the high was only about sixty degrees.

"There she is!" Fletcher roared. "My bride."

Tammy pursed her lips and clicked her tongue at Fletcher, but she obviously loved it.

"Speaking of brides," Miles dipped his drink at Logan. "You two looking to take things to the next level?"

Logan gave an awkward chortle, but he threw his gaze past the group and at Kelly, who'd sidled up next to Lucy and Mabel and had fit in seamlessly to life in the small prairie town. "Yeah." He turned back to the group. "She's the one."

Even Griffin was surprised to hear this. Not because he didn't agree—the two were a match made in heaven—but because now he had a little competition in terms of timing. "Are you going to propose soon?"

Logan asked him, "Are you?"

Griffin balked at first. Now wasn't the time. Not because he wasn't ready—he was—but because he was literally standing in front of the two men to whom he owed such a conversation.

"You know?" Tammy pointed a red-painted finger-nail toward the refreshments table. "I'm going to grab a cider." She squeezed Fletcher's arm and left.

Miles cleared his throat. "Lucy's trying to carry a chair. I'd better go intervene."

Griffin's dad hooked a thumb in the direction of his wife. "I'm thirsty, too."

"Well, look what the cat dragged in!" The familiar, craggy voice came from behind Griffin. His co-investor. Co-owner. Mentor. And many, many other things. It wasn't only Mr. Jim Kimble, though. There, too, was his son and Mabel's very own father, Norm.

Griffin had only seen Norm in passing once or twice since he'd moved to Minneapolis, and they'd exchanged little more than brief hellos or half waves. "Mr. Ryerson," he said to the younger of the two. "I heard you're coming back to Prairie Creek."

Norm, an easy-going, kind fellow, smiled and nodded. "Yep. Now that Mabel and Logan are both here, no point in us hiding out across the border." He laughed at his own joke, and Griffin took the cue to laugh, too. A line of sweat had broken out along Griffin's spine. His hands had turned clammy and his tongue had gone dry and inoperable. He found he could hardly form a response, but fortunately it was Logan who spoke next.

"Mom and Dad only ever moved because they thought I was bound to give them an heir sooner than my sister. Grandkids—that's all they care about."

"Right." Griffin nodded nervously. Did Mabel want children? Did *Griffin*? Yes. He definitely did. When they were younger, he and Mabel had fantasized about all the children they'd have, the names they'd give them, the hobbies they'd nurture. Now that it *could* be a reality, the pressure of the ticking clock thumped in Griffin's brain. "Kids," he added.

"Griffin, I know you and Mabel have really bonded these past several months. Ever since she took the leap of faith of coming here," Norm Ryerson said. If the words had come from another man, they'd fall with heavy, menacing thuds. But from Norm, they sounded like warm honey. Like the most natural conversation in the world.

Griffin rolled his shoulders back and down and tugged at his collar. "Well, sir, I can't say just how glad I am that she took that leap." If he echoed someone else's honey-sweet words maybe he wouldn't sound like the moron he felt like on the inside right about then.

"We're all happy about it." Norm looked over his shoulder, and Griffin followed his gaze to Nance Ryerson, Norm's wife. He looked back at Griffin. "I know way back when, that my in-laws—" he winked at Jim Kimble who seemed to be thoroughly enjoying this little tête-à-tête, "or at least my mother-in-law, may God rest her soul, had other ideas about you two."

Griffin pressed his lips together and just nodded. He wasn't sure whether to say that he'd agreed with Betty Kimble back then—he hadn't—or that he'd disagreed— that'd be rude, right? Instead, Griffin kept utterly quiet. He listened.

Norm went on, "I was glad she spoke her piece about it. You were both young. But Griffin," Norm put a hand on Griffin's shoulder and gave him a nice-but-serious look directly in Griffin's eyes, "we always hoped you two would end up together."

Griffin felt distinctly like he'd been betrayed. He cast a brief, calculated stare at his best friend. Logan just smirked, but it was all the confirmation Griffin needed.

It *was* time.

Chapter 30 — Mabel

Mabel was thrilled with the outcome of the day's events. While it had initially been her idea to reopen her grandparents' shop, she hadn't seen herself partaking whatsoever. But once Griffin had explained that it was Mabel's advice that drove him, well, she had jumped right in. With her enthusiasm for sewing and crafts restored, her grandfather had established a clause in the company agreement. Upon his passing, Mabel would inherit the shop. As for his other grandchildren, they'd get their own pieces of the family pie in other ways. It was fair as fair could be, and it ensured that Mabel could pursue her passion and resurrect the family legacy without the shadow of family drama looming over. Heaven knew the family didn't need any more of that.

She'd pretty much finished making the rounds at the opening party when her mother cornered Mabel. They were in the back sewing room together, after having given a small tour to the latest interested customers. Mabel and her mother hadn't spoken all too much since they'd both returned to Prairie Creek. The pain and hurt between them had lessened, to be sure, but it was Nance Ryerson's mother who was the source of the heartache, and when it came to one's own mother, all bets were off.

"Mabel," Nance held an oversize brown paper sack. It looked nearly cartoonish, and the bottom sagged heavily. Out the top of it sprung white tissue paper in pretty sprays. A gift of some order. "Have you thought of a name for the shop?"

"Oh." Mabel was surprised at this. She'd expected something more along the lines of a heart to heart as opposed to a business topic. "Well, we've got the temporary name. Kimble and Dempsey's Sew 'n' Vac."

"That's a little long, don't you think?"

Mabel looked at her mother. Maybe this wasn't a business conversation after all. "What do you mean?"

"Oh nothing." Her mother, ever a tad flighty, swiveled away and admired the room as if she hadn't already seen it. "It's great in here. Just as I remember it. A little better, I guess." She flashed her daughter a smile. Mabel braced for something. What, she didn't know.

"Mabel." Her mom looked at her with a new expression. Something between sadness and happiness. It was confusing.

Mabel tried not to roll her eyes, not because she was irritated by her mother but because she was nervous and not sure where this was going. It felt bad. Or sad. Something *not good*. Something serious.

"Honey, I want you to know that I didn't move to Minneapolis to follow Logan and run away from you."

"Okay?"

"I went there because it was hard for me to be here, too. She was my mom." Nance's voice cracked, and Mabel silently cursed the situation. It *was* sad and bad and serious. She felt the unstoppable force of tears creeping up her throat.

But her mom shook her head and wiped off the tears quickly then grabbed Mabel's hand and gave it a squeeze. "No, no. I'm not upset. I just—I just want you to know that I never felt you were at fault for what happened. I know I've told you this, but I want to say it again. I want to promise you that there is nothing in the world you can do to not make me love you. You and Logan are the lights of our lives. You were the light of Grandma's eyes, too."

Mabel could not curb the crying. It came like a lazy afternoon shower when the skies seemed blue but there had been a dark cloud hanging off in the distance all along, ready to strike just when folks thought they'd made it through another sunny day.

Her mother lifted the paper bag.

More in order to stop the tears than to see what was inside, Mabel plucked the tissue with a purpose and dove her hands into the brown paper. They caught on something wood and glass and rectangular, like a thick photo frame. She withdrew it, and though Mabel might have cried all over again, instead, she simply stared.

Affixed behind the pane of glass and neatly arranged across three shallow shelves were none other than Grandma Betty's thimbles.

Even the one with the engraving that Mabel had worn so long ago, as a little girl who'd almost never sewn again. *Kimble's Shoppe.*

* * *

After they'd hugged and wept and smiled and laughed, Nance told Mabel they could hang it out in the front of the shop as décor. Mabel preferred to keep it in the back room, though. It was where she'd spend most of her time and where she'd like to look at it. Anyway, the shadow box of thimbles was a personal, special thing. Her mother agreed readily, giving Mabel a kiss on the cheek before she went to go.

"Maybe you can think of a name that helps honor her. A name for the shop?"

Mabel nodded, and her mother left. In the moment's silence and aloneness she had, Mabel wondered what Grandma Betty would think of her now, taking up where she'd left off. Hopefully, she'd be proud. Mabel liked to think so, anyway.

A quiet knock came at the doorframe, and Mabel wiped her eyes again then looked up.

"Griff." She smiled at him. "Hey."

He didn't exactly smile back, though. "Hey."

Relief washed over her

"I have a question." She cut him off at the pass. "I'm just thinking of names for the shop. I really like the idea of calling it a shop. I mean, we're a shop, like a *work*shop —where stuff gets fixed, I know. But then again, Sew 'n' Vac is so cute, and it's what my grandparents officially named the place. I think there's a lot of value in that." She folded her arms and stared at the shadow box, which she'd propped against the wall adjacent to her main sewing table.

Griffin turned to see what she was looking at.

Mabel explained. "It's a shadowbox with the thimbles Grandma Betty collected." She hefted it up and with a finger tapped on the center thimble. "That one, see it?"

He looked, but something was a little off about Griffin. He looked pale and strange. But he managed, "Yeah?"

"Kimble's Shoppe. That's what it was originally named in the 1800s when my great-great grandfather opened it. Back then it was an actual shop-shop. They sold fabric and sewing supplies, mainly, but laundry stuff, too."

"Um, Mabel?" Griffin's face had regained color, and the new color was red.

"Griff, what's wrong?" she set the box down and took his hands, which he'd outstretched even as he licked his lips and his face flushed harder.

"Mabel, I have loved you since we were kids," he began, and she couldn't be sure where this was going.

159

"My love for you went from that to what we had when we were teenagers and all I wanted to do was make out with you behind the bleachers. But even while I wanted you to wear my Letterman's jacket and show you off to the world, I wanted to have you for other reasons. Because for everything that I'm not, you are."

Mabel's pulse raced. "Griffin—" It couldn't be. Images of movie proposals flashed through her head. Images of her own proposal from nearly a year before did, too. It was a letdown, that whole thing, perfunctory and so painfully preplanned that it was expected and unsurprising and wholly boring. She pushed it out of her head as quickly as it came. "Griffin. Are you—?"

He lowered to a knee and dug into his shirt pocket, which she was *positive* hadn't been bulging earlier in the day. "Mabel—"

"Griffin." Her eyes went wide, and she pulled one of her hands to her mouth. There was so much she could say to him right now, because for everything that Mabel wasn't, *Griffin* was. They were equals. They were best friends. They were lovers, and they were soulmates. And she could never see herself standing above him, because if there was one thing Mabel had learned in the past three years of her life, it was that you said the things you felt. You didn't wait. You didn't wait because you never knew when you were going to hit an icy patch. "Griffin, I love you," she whispered through her hand. "Is it...is it *time*?"

Griffin nodded and let go of her remaining free hand to open a small burgundy velvet box. It almost matched her blouse. He opened it and nestled in a bed of satin, not a garish, brilliant solitaire or a three-stone princess cut or anything trendy and flashy. No brand-new white gold or platinum.

And yet, it was everything Mabel could have ever wanted. It was the *only* thing Mabel could have ever wanted.

Griffin removed the family heirloom, a thin silver band with a spray of small diamonds that had to be over a hundred years old.

Grandma Betty's wedding ring.

"Mabel Elizabeth Ryerson." He looked into her eyes, and Mabel looked into his. "Will you *finally* marry me?"

She gave him her hand, and Griffin slid the ring onto her finger. Mabel felt the history of her ancestors like a ghostly hug, but she lifted her gaze to Griffin. Because in fact, while Mabel's past was important, her future was all that *really* mattered.

Her heart fluttered to life, and Mabel fell into Griffin's arms. She kissed him and hugged him and at last, after feeling the moment with all that she had, she pushed away and looked Griffin square in the eyes. "I thought you'd never ask."

"Is that a yes?" Pretend concern spread over his face.

Pure joy spread over hers. "*Yes.*"

Epilogue

October came and went, leaving behind a nip in the air. November saw changes at the shop, including a busier season—winter in South Dakota meant people had more time to sew and less tolerance for being outside. Plus, with Christmas coming, grandmothers really had better get a start on knitting hats and patching together warm winter quilts.

Mabel and Griffin had settled into their new status as an engaged couple, but they agreed on a short engagement. A winter wedding wouldn't exactly be ideal, but then again who could wait more than six months to make their love official? Not Mabel and Griff. Not a chance in the world. Their main obstacle, actually, was hunting season. Both their fathers would save weekends for pheasant hunts, and even Griffin liked to get away and get a shot at the ringnecks out on the open plains. In fact, he was hoping such a trip could work as a bachelor party, come January. Which would mean a possible wedding in February. The only thing to really think about at this point was location. In Prairie Creek, wedding venues were few and far between, and even fewer and farther between in the dead of the cold season.

After one such brainstorm session, Mabel and Griffin were both at the front desk, starting the process of closing up shop before going home to their respective domains—Griffin to his just outside of town and Mabel to hers at the newly named Country Cottage, where guests came and went faster than summer in the north.

"You want to lock the back while I go up and say goodnight to Grandpa?" Mabel asked Griffin. They both liked to leave through the front, because they could see what the place looked like to customers. It was an important part of a business, Griffin had taught her, to see your company through the eyes of others.

"Sure." He left to go to the back door, and Mabel started for the staircase, but the bell at the front rang before she could climb the first step. It was already after five. They'd already turned the sign to say *Sorry we're Closed!*

Mabel glanced back in the direction of where Griffin would be. "Somebody's here!" she called, as a matter of safety. His head popped out, and he watched her as she went to the door and opened it.

"Kelly!" she said. Kelly Watts stood there with Logan behind her, holding the handle of a hand truck. On the dolly was a large rectangular object beneath a sheet that had been tied around in twine. "What's this?"

"Your new sign!" Kelly beamed.

"Oh, of *course*!" Mabel squealed back at Griff. "Honey! It's here! The new shop sign!"

Once they commissioned Kelly to help brand the store, she'd suggested a great sign maker out of Ohio. It took only two weeks to have the sign made, shipped, and boom. Here it was.

Logan untied the twine when Griffin came out, and the two guys held it with the sheet over so that Mabel could see it as Kelly pulled off the sheet for the big reveal.

When the white fabric fell away, Mabel beamed with pride and approval. It was perfect. She read it aloud for the others. "The Thimble Shoppe." She looked gratefully at Kelly. "Thank you."

"It was my pleasure. It really is beautiful."

"The name is perfect, Mabel," Logan added. "It's a mix of Grandma Betty and you, but it leaves the door open for others after us." He said it perfectly.

"What more could you need now?" Kelly asked Mabel.

"Well, eventually, we're going to need help," she said.

"Yeah. Business is good, but we can't be here seven days a week, ten hours a day," Griff added.

"Especially with wedding planning coming up, I bet," Logan pointed out. It was cute how her brother was putting in a lot of effort to be part of Mabel and

Griffin's wedding. So cute that Mabel was beginning to wonder if there wasn't an ulterior motive.

She looked at the three of them. "Seriously, though. Do we know anyone? I have a feeling we're going to need help before the holidays hit."

Kelly crossed her arms. "You know what? I think I might know somebody."

The other three looked back at her with surprise. Logan asked, "You do?"

Kelly nodded slowly. "Actually, yeah. A good friend of mine. She's sort of in a weird place right now. Logan, do you remember my old assistant, Deb?"

Continue the saga with *A Homestead Holiday*, featuring your favorite neighbors from around Prairie Creek.

Also by Elizabeth Bromke

Prairie Creek:

The Country Cottage

The Thimble Shoppe

A Homestead Holiday

A Prairie Creek Christmas

Other Series

Heirloom Island

Harbor Hills

Birch Harbor

Hickory Grove

Gull's Landing

Maplewood

Acknowledgments

A huge thanks to my ever faithful and trusty editor, Lisa Lee. Thank you, Lisa, for polishing this baby! You are so wonderful to me. Marge Burke, your wisdom and feedback were invaluable to the cadence of this story. Thank you!

Wilette Cruz and your beautiful covers: it's thanks to you that my stories find readers! Thank you for your brilliant artistry, always.

There is a group of very special people who deserve attention here, too. My ARC team: thank you for being my earliest readers and my greatest source of encouragement! I sincerely couldn't write and publish without all of you! Thank you!

The world of Prairie Creek wouldn't be possible without one very special lady: Grandma Engelhard, thank you for everything you've given in me in my life— afternoon puzzles, bedtime stories, and a love for writing. I only hope I have your knack for pretty words, too. Finally, thank you for bringing to life the towns of Aberdeen and Milbank, South Dakota. If my settings are any good, it's all because of you. I love you so much. Thank you!

The rest of my family and friends, thank you for always offering support and love, even when I'm buried away in a fog of daydreams and writing.

Especially Ed and Eddie. My whole world!

About the Author

Elizabeth Bromke writes women's fiction and contemporary romance. She lives in the mountains of northern Arizona with her husband, son, and their sweet dogs, Winnie and Tuesday. After teaching secondary English for thirteen lucky years, she stopped teaching about stories and started writing them.

Learn more about the author by visiting her website at elizabethbromke.com.